P9-CEM-107

SHATTERING GLASS

SHATTERING GLASS

GAIL GILES

HENRY COUNTY LIBRARY SYSTEM
COCHRAN PUBLIC LIBRARY
4602 N. HENRY BLVD.
STOCKBRIDGE, GA 30281

ROARING BROOK PRESS

Brookfield, Connecticut

HENRY COUNTY LIBRARY SYSTEM
HAMPTON, LOCUST GROVE, McDONOUGH, STOCKBRIDGE

Copyright © 2002 by Gail Giles

Published by Roaring Brook Press
A division of Holtzbrinck Publishing Holdings Limited Partnership
2 Old New Milford Road, Brookfield, Connecticut 06804

All rights reserved

Library of Congress Cataloging-in-Publication Data:

Giles, Gail.
Shattering Glass / Gail Giles.
p. cm.
Summary: When Rob, the charismatic leader of the senior class,
turns the school nerd into Prince Charming, his actions
lead to unexpected violence.
[I. Popularity—Fiction. 2. High schools—Fiction. 3. Schools—
Fiction. 4. Violence—Fiction.] I. Title

PZ7.G3923 Sh 2002
[Fic]—dc21
2001041713

ISBN 0-7613-1581-0 (trade edition)
10 9 8 7

ISBN 0-7613-2601-4 (library binding)
10 9 8 7 6 5 4 3

Book design by Jaye Zimet
Printed in the United States of America

Always and always and always
For
Jim Giles and Josh Jakubik
My heroes

ACKNOWLEDGMENTS

Many thanks to: Scott Treimel *for all his work and for pairing me with the dream editor.* Deborah Brodie, *the dream editor, for her encouragement and advice. And being both a joy and an inspiration.* Simon Boughton *and all the wonderful people at Roaring Brook Press for taking a chance with me.* Nancy Werlin *for giving me the key to making this book work. Lady, you are good! Also* Cathy Atkins *and* Deb Vanasse *for reading the manuscript and giving me great advice.* Cynthia Leitich Smith *for playing midwife to the early drafts.* Bubba Strack *for helping with the salon scene and,* Josh, *I stole the Hooked on Phonics line from you. What can I say? Your mother can't be trusted if her son is that witty.* Dawn Jakubik *for marrying my son. I write better when I know he's happy. And again,* Jimmy Buffett *for writing Changing Channels.*

SHATTERING GLASS

Simon Glass was easy to hate. I never knew exactly why, there was too much to pick from. I guess, really, we each hated him for a different reason, but we didn't realize it until the day we killed him.

Simon was textbook geek. Skin like the underside of a toad and mushy fat. His pants were too short and his zipper gaped about an inch from the top. And his Fruit of the Looms rode up over his pants in back because he tucked his shirt into his tightey-whiteys. He had a plastic pocket protector, no joke, crammed with about a dozen pens and a calculator.

It was retro-cool in our part of Texas to wear loafers or Top-Sider boat shoes without socks, but Simon wore crepe-soled black lace-up wingtips.

We were all hanging in the Commons before school. Coop, as usual, was copying my English notes. Coop was our team's star linebacker and English wasn't exactly his native tongue. Sixty percent of Coop's vocabulary consisted of the word "Yo." The other forty percent was divided between "No way, man," and "I dunno." Evolution sort of passed Coop by.

The Bobster boasted of doing the wild thing with his latest girlfriend. Bob was more blow than go and we all knew it. But the guy was fun and funny and occasionally could hone in on something the rest of us missed. Besides, it was easier to put up with his bullshit than his blowouts. I had one ear cocked to Bobster while I read the big words to Coop. Rob leaned against the table watching the girls watch him. He was indifferent; the girls were not.

Last year, Rob Haynes transferred to B'Vale from out of state. Within minutes, every girl in school was tongue-hung in lust, and within days, he had snatched the popularity crown off Lance Ansley's head. There hadn't been a close contender since.

Looks-wise, Rob wasn't lacking, but that wasn't the whole story. He wore confidence like the rest us wore favorite sweatshirts. Magnetism like Rob's can't be earned. When he walked into a room, there was a jolt and all eyes turned his way. No one noticed that his nose was big, and he wasn't all that tall. His blue eyes and big smile hypnotized one and all. Rob would flash his grin, and nobody with a pulse had a chance. Girls squirmed, teachers twitched, and everyone scuffled to be first in line to give Rob whatever he wanted. And Rob let them.

Once I asked Bobster's girlfriend of the minute what was Rob's attraction. She got all gooey and sighed. "He looks right into your eyes and for a minute you're beautiful, the most important person in the world."

Rob's girl-gazing was interrupted by a shout from Lance Ansley.

"Hey! Glass!"

Rob and I looked up to see Simon Glass bumbling his way between tables.

Rob thought Lance was as useful as crotch itch. Since Ansley's vocabulary was as limited as his imagination, his habit was calling anyone in target range "faggot." Rob tensed visibly every time, and I knew that one day he'd take Lance down.

"Glass! I want to ask you something," Lance shouted above the pack.

Simon stopped, confused by Lance's attention. Surely he suspected something, but the guy was so pitifully eager. He looked around as if someone else named Glass stood behind him.

He squirmed, probably about to piss his doubleknit pants, happy to be hailed by one of B'Vale's finest. Shambling forward like a friendly seal, he nodded at Lance. "What do you need to know?"

Lance surveyed the herd of goat ropers nearby, the Goths and Tweakers, hanging on the edges like ravens at a dump site, the bangers and the preps pushed in close. Testosterone surrounded Lance like swamp gas. Standing hip-shot and relaxed, he kept his face turned slightly away from Simon. "Yeah, Glass, I got a question about your shirt."

Simon's thick eyebrows bunched together like a caterpillar. He smoothed his shirt. "What . . . what about my shirt?"

"I'm curious. Do you tuck your shirt into your jocks so it's handy to wipe your ass or what?"

A few in the roper mob hooted. Simon gulped.

Lance continued. "That shirttail was hanging there close at . . . um . . . hand?"

The laughter crossed castes now. The Goths only smiled, of course, but slapped one another on the back and jeered at Simon, glad that, this time anyway, they weren't the object of ridicule. Glass's face was crimson, and he backed away from Lance in a rush to escape. Dave Eastland stuck out one foot, snagging Simon's heels. His head and shoulders went down, and his feet flew up. He crashed and burned.

Coop shook his head. "Ansley's an asshole," he muttered. He closed his books and left.

"Later," Bob said to Rob and me, and followed Coop.

Simon lurched to his knees. As he put his hands on the floor and pushed himself up, his pocket protector spilled its contents. Pen and pencils tumbled away, and the calculator's triple A batteries scattered in all directions.

"Oh, no!" Simon wailed.

Two or three picked up the cue. "Oh, noooooo!" they shrieked. "Oh, nooooo!" The cry picked up voices and decibels as it rolled across the room.

Glass crawled on hands and knees, clutching at the wayward batteries and pens. Jeff Barnett stood, a battery resting against his shoe. As Simon reached for it, Barnett kicked, sending the triple A spinning across the floor. Simon reached for a pencil, and a foot stamped down and snapped it. Simon looked up into Lance's face.

"Sorry, Glass," he leered. "Or should I say . . . " he pitched his voice into a squeaky falsetto, "Oh, nooooo!"

Simon sighed and hung his head. Defeated.

Lance leaned over and grabbed the exposed elastic band of Glass's underwear. He stretched it out, then released. The band snapped against Simon's crack just as the bell shrieked. As the crowd moved on, one or two of them took a swipe at Simon's pens, scattering them to the far ends of the Commons. Lance picked up the calculator's plastic back and flipped it with a backhanded Frisbee toss into a garbage can. "Have a good day, Glass." He ambled off, grinning and strutting for his admirers in the crowded hall.

Rob still leaned against the table. He watched Lance leave, then turned to watch Simon gather his nerd tools and haul up his pants. He leaned down and retrieved one of Simon's pens. He strode to Glass and handed it to him. "You missed this one," he said.

Simon wouldn't take the pen. Rob slid it into Glass's shirt pocket. He turned away and jerked his chin in a signal for us to leave.

That was so Rob. While his magnetism alone was more than enough to ensure high school deification, he'd still go out of his way to be nice to someone who wasn't even a blip on the useful radar. The nobodies and the somebodies all liked him for it.

"He blew it," Rob said, smiling faintly.

"What do you expect out of Glass?" I said.

He put his hand on my shoulder. "Not Glass. Lance."

2

Glass? Rob's posse thought I was dumber than duck doo, but Glass fooled *them* not me. Simon wasn't what anybody thought he was.

—Lance Ansley

"Clue me in later. We're gonna be late," I said.

"Not a big deal." Rob strolled down the hall, unhurried.

"It *is* a big deal when Mrs. Parks gives a test. You know how she is: Start the test when the bell rings, or don't start it at all."

"We've got a sub."

"So what, Parks is bound to have left instructions."

The last bell rang as Rob spoke. "I'll handle it."

We rounded the corner to the English wing and headed to the end of the corridor.

"You two are late." The sub was babe-a-luscious, but trying not to be. She wore her long hair pulled back and a scowl on her face.

Rob stopped. "Yes, ma'am, um . . . " He flashed his

smile and shape-shifted into his humble act. "I'm really sorry. I know it's hard on a sub when you get jerks like the two of us."

"I resemble that remark," I muttered.

"We understand if you decide to write us up," Rob said.

Prepared for attitude, the sub got sideswiped. She tucked the late slips in her skirt pocket. "I . . . uh . . . no harm done, I guess. What are your names?"

"Rob Haynes, ma'am, and this is Young Steward."

She checked her roll sheet, then chewed her bottom lip. "I see Haynes, Rob, but I don't—"

I interrupted. "Look for Thad."

She rescanned. "Young? That's an unusual nickname, isn't it?"

Groans drifted around the room. Too many had heard the story too many times.

"It's a long and boring story—" I began.

"Believe him," an Honor Society drone drawled from the last row.

Rob cut in. "Young is really Thaddeus R. Steward IV. His great granddad was Thad, his granddad is Junior, his dad is Trey, so . . ." He gave her his I'm-as-cute-as-a-fuzzy-little-duckling smile. "The family kept with Roman numerals but"—Rob leaned in to whisper—"didn't want to call him Little Steward. Bad for a guy's self-image. Hence, the Young Steward."

The sub shook her head, grinning. "Take your seats, please. You have a test to take."

"Mrs. Parks usually gives us fifteen minutes to review before vocabulary tests," Rob said. "Is that cool with you?"

The sub pulled wisps of hair toward her face. "Sounds like a good idea. No problem."

Rob sauntered down the aisle. I followed and eased into my seat. In twenty minutes he had the sub off on a jag about her recommendations for college or some other bull shit and there was no time for Mrs. Parks's marathon vocab test.

As we left class, Todd Carter stopped Rob. "Way cool."

"Glad to be of service," Rob said.

"Parks will crap hot coals when she hears the sub did-n't give the test," I said. "That babe won't be subbing here again."

"Not my problem," Rob said.

"Does an instruction manual come with being your friend? One minute you worry about Simon Glass's pen and next you put a sub out of work."

"The sub did what I wanted. Game over. I won."

"And Glass?"

Rob grinned. "That game's just beginning."

"I hate it when you do your Mystery Man bullshit."

"No, you don't."

"And I hate it when you do that, too," I said.

Rob grinned. "Young, about the sub? Didn't you notice the honker-size diamond on the babe's ring finger?

Do you think she wants a career of substitute teaching?"

All my mind could think was "duh?"

"And if she does, she's lousy at it." Rob turned to Mia Deacon as she strolled past. "Mia, new haircut? Lookin' good!" She smiled and her fingertips strayed to her bangs.

Rob morphed back to our conversation. "We saved the educational system and the babe a lot of time and trouble. If she ever remembers me, she'll thank me."

Even when I allowed myself a fleeting suspicion that Rob was wrong, he made so much sense that I had to follow his lead. We all followed. He made it easy.

Later, Rob and I pushed our orange plastic trays along the aluminum rails of the lunch line. Coop trailed behind. "What is this stuff?"

Rob groaned. "Hamster litter?"

"Used hamster litter," I added.

"I think it's salad," Coop said. "I'll eat it if you don't want it."

"You'd eat the trays, Coop." I picked up the Jell-O. "Solid as a rock. I think they fill holes in the parking lot with this stuff."

"What's the main dish?" Rob asked the square-bodied cafeteria worker.

"Lasagna." She gave Rob a don't-start-with-me look.

"What's in it?" I asked.

"Wet paper towels, Alpo, and melted vinyl," Rob answered.

"Yours has an added attraction," Big Block Body said, slapping a chunk of lasagna on Rob's plate. "I spit on it." She didn't smile.

"Here, Coop," Rob said. "It's yours."

"What are you gonna eat?" Coop asked.

Rob waggled his eyebrows at the disgruntled woman. "My words."

"Good choice," she shot back.

"There's one that's not hot for you," I said.

"Gotta be blind," he said.

We moved down the line and grabbed our desserts.

"What did you mean this morning when you said Lance had messed up?" I asked.

"Dork-baiting is amateur hour. What's the challenge making Glass look stupid? Lance didn't prove anything except he's desperate for attention."

"I guess, but—"

"That's not real power; true power would be making the sheep *like* Simon." He paused and then grinned like he had just tasted something surprisingly good. "Want to test it? Make Glass Joe Popular."

"Yeah, right."

Rob smiled, twining his way through a few tables. "Jen, save me a seat next to you during Eco, will you? Amos, how's your knee, you going to be able to play

Friday?" He knew names. He knew what mattered to each person he met.

He scanned the cafeteria. In the corner sat Simon Glass, alone at a table for ten, hunched over a brown paper sack, eating what looked like a bologna sandwich.

"Watch and learn, good buddy." Rob cruised straight for Simon. "Hey, Glass. Mind company?"

Simon looked up, hunched further, and pulled his milk carton closer to his chest. No doubt he was full up on friendliness from the hot shots today.

I stood, hesitating, next to Rob. Coop rolled up behind me.

"Relax, Glass," Rob whispered. "Sit up straight, smile, and invite me to sit down."

Simon bolted upright. "Sure, have a seat." As he spoke, half-chewed bread wads hung off his bottom lip.

"Thanks, man." Rob gestured for us to sit. "Save a place for Bobster. He's still in line." He sat next to Simon. Rob couldn't have attracted more attention if he had set off firecrackers and danced naked on the tabletop. The place got almost quiet. I sat across the table. Coop looked confused as usual, but just dug into his lasagna. "This ain't bad," he announced. "She didn't really spit on it."

"We rely on Coop," Rob told Simon, smiling. "He's our taste tester. If his pupils don't dilate, we know he's not poisoned."

Simon eyed Rob, then looked long and hard at me, then at the oblivious Coop.

"Glass, I think Lance was a real shit this morning,"
Rob said.

Simon looked up, anticipating the sucker punch.

"No shit. You were man enough to ignore him. Like
he was crap on your shoes."

Simon blinked.

"Young said the same thing. Didn't you, Young?"

Here I was being dragged into another Rob program.
I'd noticed Ronna Perry watching. "Yeah." I cleared my
throat and shot Rob a look of disgust. "I . . .um . . .
thought you made him look like a jackass. Course, that's
not such a stretch for Lance."

Simon took a bite of his sandwich. I was wrong. PBJ.

"Young, you gonna eat your cake?" Coop was well
into his feeding frenzy.

I handed it over.

"What do you want, Rob?" Simon's voice was a
wheeze.

Rob smiled and gave Simon the once-over. "There's
more to Simon Glass than we know, isn't there?"

Simon lifted his chin. His bland face showed glim-
mers of defiance. "Maybe."

"That's good; it'll be easier."

"What are you guys talking about?" Coop asked,
reaching for my milk. I batted his hand away.

Rob laughed and shoved his milk to Coop. Looking
up, he waved. "Bobster. Over here."

Bobster nodded and started toward us. Catching

sight of Simon Glass, he hesitated in mid-stride. Rob waved again. Bobster shook his head but continued. His foot hooked the chair rung to pull it out.

"Hey, Rob." He nodded to us. "Coop, Young." He paused, lowered his voice, "Glass?"

"I've got a deal to discuss with Glass, Bobster. I was just getting around to it."

Simon wadded up his sandwich wrapper. He dragged on the last of his milk through the straw and pushed it in the bag. "I have to go now," he said. "Computer lab."

"Sure. Talk to you later, Glass?"

Simon brushed his nose with the back of his wrist. "I guess," he stammered. He waited a half-minute, looking anxious. Why not? Most eyes in the lunchroom were locked on him. "Sure, Rob," he said louder. "We'll talk later." He crunched his lunch bag into a compact wad, dropped it squarely in the garbage, and pushed the swinging door. I saw him smooth his hair as the door swung back.

3

It's been five years since that night in the gym. What you don't understand is that he helped me. Maybe what he and the others did changed my plans for the future, but he's paid for that in more than one way. The future I have now is a good one and I wouldn't have it without him. So, sure I'm going to help him now. It's what a decent person does.

—Jeff Cooper

After school, the four of us worked out in the weight room. I spotted Coop lifting a barbell that weighed approximately the same as a '57 Buick. Rob glided on the rowing machine, and Bobster curled free weights in front of the mirror.

Coop spoke as he lifted. "What's this, *huff,* deal, *huff,* you're making with, *huff,* Glass?"

Rob eased his legs out. "We turn Simon Glass into Prince Charming." He swiped his dripping forehead with a towel, then tossed it at Bobster.

Bobster kicked the towel, eyes fixed on the mirror. "Cut it out, I'll lose count."

Bobster put one weight against his hip, turned slightly sideways, and raised one weight in an overhand grip, tightening his biceps into a muscle-man pose. "This is primo male flesh. Can a foldout in Playgirl be far behind?"

"I hear when they put the staple in your dick it hurts like hell," I said.

Bobster dropped the dumbbell and shot me the bone. I helped Coop cradle the barbell and he sat up. "No way, man. They don't do that."

Picking up the towel, Bobster wrapped it around Coop's face. He sat on a bench opposite Rob. "What is this crap about Glass anyway? No offense, man, but . . ." he paused, searching for words. "The guy's a full-goose Magoo."

A *full-goose Magoo?* It had to be bad. When Bob couldn't think of a phrase, he made them up. I kept a list, *The Book of Bob*.

Coop and I flopped on the slant boards and started sit-ups.

Rob moved to the butterfly machine. He sat, adjusted the tension, hooked his forearms behind the pads, pulled them together, and released.

"That's the point. Making Glass popular is a true challenge." He pressed the pads together and released. "And I *loves* a challenge." He looked like a kid with a Christmas present.

"Might be fun," Bobster said. "Like that Pig story we read in English."

Rob looked to me to translate.

"He means *Pygmalion*," I said. "Come on, Coop, let's hit the showers. If you want help with that research paper."

Coop stood and slung his towel around his neck. "It would be cool to help Glass. I feel sorry for him."

Coop's three mutts bolted from under the sagging front porch and hit the cracked and oil-stained driveway, wiggling and wagging, overjoyed that their master was home. I was explaining the difference between footnotes and endnotes as we banged through the screened door of his kitchen and dumped our books on the littered table. One glance said it all. A long time since a woman had lived here.

"Coop." A slurred, raspy voice bellowed.

Coop grimaced. "Caveman is home." He moved to the doorway between the kitchen and den. "Yeah? What is it, Dad?"

"Get your lazy butt in here."

Coop trudged into the small, dark room. I saw the muscles in his jaw bunch.

Coop's dad sprawled in a recliner. His enormous bulk sagged over the sides. He wore old paint-stained khakis and a dirty, ribbed undershirt. A roll of fat escaped from between the bottom of the undershirt and the top of the pants. The pants were unbuttoned to accommodate his bulging waist. The recliner tilted back and the fat on his arms drooped on the vinyl when he lifted his arm to guzzle his beer.

"Find the remote. I wanna watch *The Simpsons*." He crumpled the aluminum can and dropped it. It joined the pile by his chair. "Another dead soldier," he grunted. "Go get me a live one."

Coop fetched the beer and the remote.

"What's Young doing here?"

The tension in Coop's jaw extended and corded his neck. I shot Coop a don't-worry-about-it look. "I'm helping Coop with his research paper, Mr. Cooper."

Mr. Cooper snorted; he wiped his lips with the back of a meaty hand. "Lotta good that'll do him. All he'll ever do is win trophies for lettin' people run into him." He gestured to a covey of gold statuettes on the television. "I won trophies, too. Fullback. All District. Not good enough for a scholarship. Ended up pumpin' gas for a livin'. He will too. Just like his old man. Big and stupid." His words droned down. His eyes blinked, then closed, then blinked again. "Get outta here."

Coop was gone. I looked in the kitchen but found him in his room, shuffling his note cards.

A framed photograph stood on a nightstand. The

woman had dark red hair; a snub nose; big, round, dark
eyes; and a mischievous grin. Coop looked just like her,
right down to a slightly crooked front tooth that made
him resemble a happy, overgrown first grader. Coop's eyes,
though, didn't glint with her quirky intelligence.

Coop's mom was the bouncy cheerleader who mar-
ried the high school gridiron star. He went to seed and
she took off. Smart enough to vamoose, she was cold
enough to leave Coop. He and his dad were too much
alike.

"He's full of it, Coop. You'll get a scholarship. You've
been scouted by every university around."

"If I don't pass English, I won't get shit. And a torn
tendon, a broken bone, anything, and I'll be digging ditch-
es for the county or . . . " he swallowed and muttered—
"pumping gas." He buried his face in the black-and-white
ruff of the dog that had crept onto the bed.

"English is *my* thing. I can write this paper standing
on my head and farting Dixie. Listen to Young the
Magnificent and don't break your leg. If you do, we'll
shoot you like a horse." I punched Coop's shoulder, trying
to cheer him.

"Might as well," he said. "Dead's better than pumping
gas."

I saw the fear in his face.

"You aren't him, Coop."

He forced a grin. "Right."

"And you aren't John Keats, either, but you have to do a critical analysis of his poems, wuss. Let's lock and load." My words bounced off the grimy Sheetrock walls and echoed down the hollow hall.

4

I didn't talk about it then. I don't talk about it now. What's
five years? I won't be talking about it in twenty-five years.
What happens to Young now, happens. I'm not involved.
—Bob DeMarco

Coop, Bobster, and I met Rob in the Commons the next
morning. Doors on the west side were open and the nutri-
tionally obsessed got orange juice, granola, and fruit. Most
of us stocked up on cinnamon rolls, Ho Hos, and Cokes.
Loungers and crammers crowded the long tables. Bobster
shepherded Coop through the intricacies of an Algebra
assignment. Rob sat behind two packages of powdered
doughnuts. He flipped one package on its end, flipped it
again while he eyed the glass front doors and chatted up
the passersby. Sighting his prey, he strode across the
Commons without a word.

Simon Glass shifted from one foot to the other next
to the barriers that closed off the corridors until the first
bell. Rob said something to Glass, who looked back at us
and shook his head. Rob grinned, spoke again, placed his

hand on Simon's shoulder, and guided him through the maze of tables. Few disguised their stares.

When they arrived at the table, Rob pulled out a chair across from Bob, Coop, and me, and gave Simon a nudge. Glass thumped down, holding himself crunched together and shifting his eyes to see if anyone was watching. Rob straddled a chair backward and pushed a package of the doughnuts to Simon.

Bob and Coop paused in their pursuit of Algebra to watch. I browsed my Lit text as if uninterested. Ronna Perry was two tables over. She wasn't looking, but she might start.

"Consider this a power breakfast," Rob said, popping the cellophane on his package of doughnuts.

Simon reached for the doughnuts, then hesitated. "What's the deal, Rob? You just woke up this morning and decided Simon Glass was your best buddy?"

"Settle down, Simon," Rob said, surprised that Simon had any punch in him. "Nobody's going to do anything to you." He smiled, warm and welcoming, and twirled a sugary doughnut on the end of his index finger. "Like I said yesterday, you're smarter than they know."

Simon swiped at his nose.

"Simon, you can't let them treat you like the class goat anymore. Your days of being a mook are numbered."

"Right, Rob."

Rob leaned forward. His voice dropped to a smooth

whisper. "Don't *ever* doubt me, Glass." He slid the doughnuts closer to Glass. When Rob smiled, Simon was daz-
zled by the light. He was human after all. "Now, do you
want that?"

Glass looked at each of us in turn, then back at Rob.
He put one finger on the package of doughnuts and eased
in. His wheezy voice barely escaped his lips. "Maybe I do."

Rob slapped the table and stood. "Let's go someplace
private."

"Wait." Simon was still hunched, the doughnuts now
in his hands. "What's in this for you?"

Rob aimed his index finger at Simon. The sugary
doughnut remained impaled. He cocked his thumb like a
pistol hammer and pushed it down. It hit the doughnut,
shearing through one side. Sugar exploded and the doughnut dropped onto the tabletop. The pieces rolled toward
Simon.

"Satisfaction," Rob said. He blew on his finger as if
he'd fired a gun.

5

Why was Rob popular? In a small public school if you're okay to look at, have enough money to dress, and have minimum social skills, you're in the top ten percent. Then anyone who is the alpha wolf takes over. We'd been a little sick of Lance for a while and ready for a new alpha male. You'd think Bob would have taken over, but Bob was more a sheep in wolf's clothing. Rob came in and just took over the lead. And we followed because that's what the rest of the pack does. Rob's dark side? Sure, I knew he had one, anyone with that many secrets . . . . And Young? Rob hooked him and reeled him in. I think Young was so blinded at being Rob's "chosen" that he couldn't see when it started to go so wrong. But Rob was the sun and you have to want to travel a long way to find the dark side of the sun. Simon, though, he let Rob show him how to dress and behave, but he never lost himself in Rob. You know, I didn't either. There was a cold center in Rob. Where his heart should have been. I feel like I should have explained that to Young, warned him.

—Blair Crews

Rob laughed, and drummed the table. "Simon, I get off on a challenge. I get pissed when the herd pushes one of the weak out. I don't want *them* to say who stays and who gets shit on. I want to even up the score."

Coop nodded. "Yeah, we're gonna stop people from bullying you. It ain't right when some loser . . . " Coop stopped. He looked down at his papers. "It ain't right."

Bob rubbed his chin in mock thought. "Besides, I need someone to comfort the babes I dump. All those suicide threats get old."

I was silent.

Rob drummed the table. "That's it." He turned to us and nodded.

Simon cut his eyes to Rob. There was no bumbling or confusion in his glance. Simon was calculating, sorting the debits from the credits. But something else. Something that said *more*, but I didn't know what kind of *more* it was. What didn't we know about this guy? Simon saw me watching him and *poof* the mook was back.

"Let's go." Rob stood. Coop copied a final answer from Bobster's paper and shoveled it into his overstuffed notebook.

"Hey, give my homework back. Once it's in that mess, I'll never see it again," Bobster said.

Coop handed Bobster the paper and shoved the bulging notebook under his arm. "You ain't wrong. Half the zeros I get are for papers I did but lost."

"Correction, papers you *copied* but lost," Rob said. He tugged one of the flapping sheets of notebook paper hanging haphazardly from Coop's binder.

"This vocabulary is from three weeks ago." Rob looked at Simon. "Maybe Glass can help you, Coop."

Rob took off toward the back of the gym. Looking around, he pulled a key from his pocket and unlocked a door at the end of a small, dark corridor between the gyms and the swimming pool. The equipment room. "Step into my office." He grinned as he ushered us in. "I somehow found myself in possession of a master key. Nobody's here until athletics classes, sixth period."

The equipment room was small and square with walls and floors of cement. Stacks of mats lined the wall opposite the door. Racks of balls, boxes of timers, standing racks of golf clubs and baseball bats were stashed semi-neatly.

"Great." Coop stretched out full-length, resting his head against a rolled tumbling mat. Bob leaned against the stacked mats and I sat on top of them. Simon stood in the middle of the open space between the door and the mats.

Glass shifted from foot to foot. "We're . . . uh . . . uh . . . we're not supposed to be in here."

Rob settled against a stack of sand-filled canvas bases. Folding his arms across his chest, he said, "Glass, you're changing from pond scum to popular. We'll all help you out. So, if you can do some small favors in return, well, that's what friends are for. Right?"

"I knew there was a catch."

"No catch, Glass. Don't do anything you don't want to do."

Simon didn't answer.

"First off. There's not much we can do today, but . . . " Rob tossed something from his jacket pocket. "We can start with this."

Simon fumbled the catch and dropped the dark object that flew at him. He leaned over and picked it up. "A comb?"

"Yeah, a comb," Bob said.

"You need a good haircut, but at least straighten it up for now," Rob said.

Simon tugged the comb through his briar patch.

"Ditch the wingtips," Bob said.

"And zip your pants," Coop added. "The babes call you 'Peek-a-Pecker.'"

Glass clutched at his crotch and flushed. He jerked on the tab of his zipper. "It won't stay up."

"That's because your pants are too tight, and you don't push the tab against the tracks to lock it," Bobster said.

Glass peered down at his pants.

We all traded rolling-eye glances.

"Glass, are you from Mars, or what?" Coop asked, cradling the back of his neck in his hands. "The Gap could fix half your problems."

"Glass likes to have it his own way." Rob cocked his head. "Right, Simon? A little passive-aggressive rebellion?"

Glass could have been statuary for all the reaction he showed.

Rob laughed. "That's what's in it for me, Simon. I like a rebel."

"Coop," Rob said. "Why don't you set Glass up on an exercise program? Let's lose a little flab, huh, Simon?"

"Get your shirttail out of your jocks." I leaned back on my elbows. "And lose the pocket protector."

Simon pulled the calculator and pens out of his pocket and bobbed his head.

"Saturday, you need to get some new clothes," Rob said.

"These are new."

"Where do you get them?" Bobster asked. "Geeks-R-Us?"

"In fact," Rob continued, "lets make a day of it. Clothes, haircut, shoes, the works. You got money for all this?"

Simon said, as if insulted, "I've got a credit card."

Bobster snorted. "He spends money to dress like this? I don't know, Rob, he could be hopeless."

"I don't think so." The first bell rang. Rob opened the door and led Simon out, one hand on his shoulder. "What do you think, Glass?"

Simon squared his shoulders and pulled the gap of his shirt over his stomach. "I don't think so, either."

And then Simon Glass did something I'd never seen him do.

He smiled.

When Rob came to B'Vale, I was the stud monkey here. Next thing I knew, I'd lost my girlfriend and my place on top. But for Rob that wasn't enough. He's one of those guys that wouldn't piss on you if you were on fire. He wasn't happy to have it all, he had to make sure I didn't have anything.

—Lance Ansley

My first sight of Rob Haynes was the day he entered B'Vale last year. He breezed into Ms. Terhune's Honors English class, handed over his papers, and took a seat. As he passed my desk, I caught sight of an oversized paperback book resting on top of his Lit text. *The Duke of Deception,* by Geoffrey Wolff. Since most readers in my class considered Grisham, King, and Danielle Steel great literature, I took a second look.

We were taking a quiz, so he read. I wondered if this was all for show.

After the bell rang, I stood at my desk until Rob passed. "Hey, I noticed your book."

Rob's look appraised me. "It's great. If you haven't read it, give it a try."

I liked that. He tested me without insulting my intelligence. I smiled. "Read it. Yeah, it's good. Did you read his brother's book?" Hey, I could test, too.

"*This Boy's Life*?" He nodded, passing the test. This guy had definite potential. Bob was smart, but an engineer-in-training smart. Coop was strictly Hooked On Phonics.

"When do you have lunch?" I asked.

Rob pulled out his schedule. "After fourth." He handed me his schedule.

"We have Government together. Why don't you eat with my buddies and me? Guess they told you this place is a closed campus and we have to eat in the cafeteria. I can introduce you around."

I introduced Rob to Coop and Bobster. Rob zeroed in on the right questions and soon he had them spilling their stories. When the bell rang, he stood. "If you guys don't have plans, why don't we meet at Biggie's Pizza tonight? You can give me the real deal about B'Vale. I don't want to make an ass of myself finding out on my own."

Coop, Bob, and I were like most guys. We'd get together and it was the I-don't-know game:

"Want to go someplace?"

"Sure."

"Where?"

"I don't know. Where do you want to go?"

"I don't care. You decide."

It could go on until Alaska melted.

Rob had circumvented the routine. He gave us a place and a plan. We were random stars, and he made us a constellation.

After classes, I spun by the library. Scrounging the stacks, I caught a glimpse of Rob. I maneuvered my way to the open catwalk until I could see what he was reading. The yearbooks. All the books were opened to the "popularity posse" pages. Names of the Class Faves, Homecoming candidates, Prom Queen and King.

We were in those pages for different reasons. The big gun was Lance Ansley. He came from oil money and was considered good-looking. He played football and basketball, so he had the jock vote, but he hung with the kickers. Widespread appeal. He'd won every popularity contest since he'd gotten out of diapers.

Coop was there because he was a football god. Strong of body and of heart, Coop was too damn nice not to like. Bob was fun and affected females like catnip. Coop and I hung with him because he liked us. I made those yearbook pages by default. My family's wealth and social and political connections could've thrown me into goober territory, except I had even features and good hair. All I had to do was not offend anyone. And I lived in fear that I'd be found out for the fraud I was.

I passed off Rob's taking notes of B'Vale's Who's Who as the new guy making sure he didn't get sucked into the wrong crowd. Slime balls are always the most welcoming. And while it made me admire the guy for taking control of his own destiny, I didn't mention it to Bob and Coop.

A couple of weeks later, Rob and I were in Advanced Bio, waiting for Mr. Tannen.

He came in, toting a cumbersome box dotted with small holes. The box shook and vibrated; muffled croaks drifted out.

Each of us perched on a tall stool at our station. Tall jars with screw-on lids sat on the lab bench in front of us. Diagrams of eviscerated life-forms decorated the dingy beige walls.

Mr. Tannen slid the box onto his desk. "Noisy little buggers," he groused, wiping his hands. "Hope no one has been snacking. I hate puke in my classroom." He pointed to the dissecting tools. "Slice-and-dice day, kids."

I groaned. I hated this crap. I hated the smell, the attitude, the gory diagrams.

"You might be wondering why we have live frogs. In regular Bio you get a dead frog preserved in formaldehyde, but that discolors your specimen. Plus, a newly devitalized animal will have nerve and muscular reaction. We'll examine these reactions today."

He peered over his horn-rim glasses. "I hope there are no faint-of-hearts or budding antivivisectionists in here. This is an elective course. No one will be excused."

The frogs croaked. Apparently they wished to be excused.

Tannen hefted the box and wove through the lab stations. Dropping a frog in each opened jar, he chatted and made friendly. Like some game show Host of Death.

"Mr. Steward, you look as green as your amphibious amigo."

"You do look like crap." Rob slid his frog out of its jar. Sitting on Rob's opened palm, its white throat bulged and its froggy eyes popped. Fat and wet, it sat humped up and tense.

"You'll find a tray of cotton balls soaked in chloroform at the end of each table. Get two. Please be sure to use the tongs. Put the cotton balls in the jar with your animal and secure the lid."

Rob lifted the frog to eye level. "He reminds me of somebody." The frog gave a rolling *Garruuuump* and sprang from Rob's hand. It hit the table with a splat, then bunched and leaped, long legs trailing.

"Catch him, Young."

I snagged the frog in mid-leap and returned it to Rob. His chiseled features clouded. He snatched the frog and squeezed until the frog's eyes goggled. He placed his index finger against the pad of his thumb and flicked it, striking the frog on its puffed throat. It made a dull, wet smack. "I'll teach you to try and get away." Another sharp flick and another, louder smack.

I knew Rob was just goofing, but it made my Cheerios curdle. "Cut it out, Rob, this isn't serial killer training camp."

"Mr. Haynes." Tannen appeared at Rob's elbow. "Can you stop playing with your specimen? You are to devitalize it, not make a pet." He pinched a dripping cotton ball with the tongs, handed one to Rob and another one to me.

My mouth dried, and my tongue felt thick. Swallowing hard, I looked at my frog, which sat unaware, blinking slowly, puffing his milky throat in and out.

I licked my parched lips and grasped the tongs tight between my fingers. The cotton ball dribbled in a thin stream down the tongs to my wrist and soaked into my cuff—its rank, cloying, sweet smell making my eyes water.

From behind me, Tannen's hand snaked out, grabbed the tongs, and tossed another cotton ball into the jar. He dumped the tongs in the sink, then screwed the lid down tight. "Courage, Mr. Steward. He doesn't feel a thing."

The frog jumped wildly against the glass. My break-fast rising, I turned and stared out the window.

I heard lids slapping.

"Mr. Haynes, put your animal in the receptacle and stop horsing around." I turned to see Rob, still holding his frog, pressing the sopping cotton ball over its face. The frog's back legs paddled against Rob's arm.

"*Now,* Mr. Haynes." Tannen's annoyance flavored the word. "And you two be sure to wash your hands thoroughly. This stuff will kill you. Ask the frogs."

Rob dropped the frog and the cotton into the jar and capped it. He leaned his arms on the table and rested his chin on his forearms. His face was rapt, engrossed in the frog's slowing movements.

I looked out the window again and concentrated on the yellowing leaves and the scudding clouds. I knew the frog was dead when I heard Rob's hushed, exultant whisper.

"Awesome!"

My gut roiled at the sight of the glistening muscles and the flayed skin. I prodded where I was told to prod, and tasted something sour when the dead frog twitched in response. Afterward I scrubbed the smell away.

"Young, you're scrubbing the skin off."

I dried my red, raw hands and gathered my books. "Let's get the hell out of Dodge."

Rob didn't speak until we got to our lockers. "I don't think Biology is your thing, Young. You need to bail."

"Right. I'm supposed to take life advice from a sadist."

"Sadist? Since when?"

"You were torturing that frog."

Rob shook his head. "You're not a frog, so I think you're safe."

Safe.

7

Of course we wondered why these boys were so suddenly Simon's friends. But we were delighted that Simon was coming out of his shell. He became interested in how he looked, he didn't lock himself up in his room with his computer, he seemed happy. And how could we suspect something like this would happen? That Steward boy. His father's a doctor and on the school board. His uncle was a State Representative. That family has always been respected in this town. Bob's father works for the same firm I do. We didn't know anything about the other boy, Rob, but he was charming and had lovely manners. What could we have done?

—Diane Glass

I was voted designated driver for Saturday's spree because I had the best car, a slightly used 4 x 4 Jeep Cherokee, sturdy and sedate enough to please my father and quietly flash enough for me. Bobster and Coop came to my house; we picked up Rob and headed for Simon's.

"Anybody know where Glass lives?" I asked.

Rob yelled from the backseat. "Six-twenty-seven Timberlake Drive."

"Timberlake, pretty uptown," Bobster said.

Coop spoke up. "His parents are big Dow execs, both of them. Into the status thing. You know, good address, the right cars, two computers, and one kid."

"How do you know?" Rob asked.

"After school, we shot the shit. He took my notebook home with him."

"He needed to start a fire?" Bobster asked.

"Dunno. He just asked to borrow it."

That was Coop. He'd probably lend his underwear if someone asked him for it. Six-twenty-seven Timberlake Drive was a sprawling one-story house nestled on the lake. Landscaped and manicured, it shouted good architect and stacks of cash.

"Not bad!" Bobster whistled. "This guy's as rich as you are, Young."

We tramped up a brick path. The front door was massive, and its glass side panels gleamed. Rob rang the bell and the door ripped open. Had Glass been lying in wait? Hair combed; shirt pocket empty; his pants—khakis showing a mile of sock—pressed; Simon grinned.

Bobster shouldered past Simon. "This place is great!"

"Come in, look around if you like," Glass mumbled.

"We like," Bobster said. We entered a marble foyer with a high vaulted ceiling. A huge chandelier glittered overhead. Glass led us to a high-tech kitchen that gleamed with antiseptic whiteness.

"What's this way?" Bob pointed to a hall.

"That's my wing."

"Your wing?" Coop asked.

"My parents told the architect to design the house so they wouldn't have to hear my music. Their bedroom, study, and library are there, and mine is on this side." He showed us down a hall lined with abstract paintings.

Coop's house would fit in Simon's bedroom. A connecting room held a big-screen TV, a VCR, a DVD, a sound system, and computer paraphernalia that would make the Pentagon jealous. Shelves crammed with books, model rockets, and microscopes filled the walls, and a telescope as big as a howitzer stood in a corner.

"I'd put a weight bench in here," Coop said.

"You never have to see your parents in this place," I said.

"I almost never do see my parents. I spend all of my time on the computer and stuff."

Glass relaxed. He had something we admired. The mood changed when Bobster opened the closet. "This is unbelievable."

We inspected the closet. Five pairs of navy blue, double-knit slacks and six or seven shirts hung there, all white or pale blue.

"This is it?" Bobster demanded.

Simon ducked his head. "I've got these khakis and this plaid shirt." He was pointing to the clothes he wore. "My grandmother gave them to me for my birthday."

Rob clapped Simon on the shoulder. "Glass, the clothes rebellion is over. You gotta dress for success. That's what we're here for—renovations."

"Major renovations," Bobster muttered, closing the door on the offending sight. "Burn all that crap or bury it."

Simon got his wallet, checked his credit cards, and squeezed the billfold into the back pocket of his straining khakis. We piled in and pointed my Cherokee toward Houston's Galleria. Coop sang along with the radio and imitated static when he couldn't remember the words.

Rob and Bobster sat in the back bucket seats, while Simon wobbled on the hump between them. They discussed Simon's new look.

Coop was a jeans, T-shirt, and athletic shoes guy, by the demands of his limited wallet and lifestyle. But Bob dressed. Long and lean, dark and handsome, Bob traded on his looks. He wore linen slacks in summer and soft wool or flannel dress slacks in winter. He made clothes look good rather than the other way around. Rob and I were middle of the sartorial road.

"I think we ought to forget about a fashion statement," Rob said.

Simon swiveled his head toward Rob and opened his mouth, "I think—"

Bob interrupted. "Gotta go casual, but not sloppy."

Simon swung toward Bob, opened his mouth again.

But Rob spoke. "Semiprep might do it. Kind of Eddie Bauer, L. L. Bean, or Banana Republic."

Simon gave up and stared straight ahead.

"Tees and bags won't work," I said.

Bobster gave a mock shiver. "No way."

Simon's head swiveled as we hashed out his shortcomings and a plan of attack. In forty-five minutes, we had ideas and a parking spot.

As we bailed, Rob pointed to the driver's side mirror. "Glass, take a last look. And say goodbye."

Simon looked, then glanced at each of us, unsure. He looked back to Rob.

"Trust me." Rob smiled.

We took off for the mall entrance. Simon tore his eyes away from his reflection and followed, gathering speed as he caught up.

The Galleria's three floors of upscale stores, plus four-star hotels, were covered with a glass dome. Trees grew in mammoth pots, fountains sprayed in arches, and the centerpiece was an ice rink, the biggest of the few on the Texas Gulf Coast.

We gave Glass's credit card a healthy workout. We traveled from store to store to store, level to level, piling up khaki pants, pleated and cuffed, measured to break at the tops of his shoes. We got button-down cotton shirts in stripes, plaids, and solids. Jeans, vertical-striped rugby jerseys, boat shoes and loafers, sweats, running shoes, a leather bomber jacket, and dark crew-necked sweaters completed the haul.

"One more thing," Simon said. He barged into a sporting goods store and past aisles of fishing rods and tennis rackets. He snagged a dark blue nylon backpack. "This, too," he said, smiling and proud.

"Good." Rob slung the pack by one strap over Simon's left shoulder. "Remember, one shoulder."

Simon all but wagged his tail. "Sure, one strap."

"Now the hair," Bobster said.

We cruised to a place called Scizzorhandz.

Shiny chrome and scads of mirrors announced a salon that catered to the young and fashionable, rather than blue-haired geezer-ladies. We flipped through magazines and watched MTV in the waiting room until the nose-and-eyebrow-pierced receptionist said, "Dragon will see you now."

Dragon?

Dragon eyeballed us and pointed to Simon. "This *must* be the client." He seated and sheeted Glass before any of us could manage a sound. Dragon had blue spiked hair and a tattoo that crawled from his neck to his cheek.

Rob said, "Nothing weird. Neat, preppie short, you know."

The stylist rolled his eyes. "Come back in forty minutes," he commanded. "Y'all make me nervous, shoo, shoo!" He flapped his manicured hands at us and squinted at Glass's hair with deadly intent. He parted it to the left, to the right, and spied us watching. He placed one hand on his hip and spoke to our reflections. "I won't do a thing until you leave. I must concentrate."

We took Simon's packages to the car and went to get root beer and chocolate chunk cookies. Hanging over the rails, we watched the ice skaters circle, twirl, and leap across the rink below us. The female skaters wore tight, stretchy dresses with short, flippy skirts.

"Think of all those hours of practice," I said.

"Perfect control," said Rob.

"Cool moves," said Bobster.

"Great legs, great butts," said Coop.

"That's what we meant," Rob said.

"Voilá!" the stylist trilled. He spun the chair and whisked the drape with a flourish, unveiling Simon. Amazing. Glass's hair lay against his head from a perfectly straight part. And he had two separate eyebrows.

"I thinned out the brows and pulled the hair forward. He has such a high forehead." Dragon clucked. "Now you can see his lovely eyes."

Bobster punched Rob. "His lovely eyes."

"Glass, my man." Rob walked around the chair, nodding and smiling. "This is getting easier by the minute."

Simon popped out of the chair, checked his reflection, then slapped his hands together. "What happens now?"

I got home late. We toured the Galleria until Simon's credit card threatened a meltdown. Simon paid for dinner at Outback Steakhouse and the latest action flick. We carried packages into his house and found a note taped to his bedroom door.

"Out to dinner and theater." No signature. Simon pitched it into a wastebasket.

"Coop," Simon wheezed. "I have something for you." He picked up a black notebook from his desk and thrust it at Coop.

"What's this?" Coop grunted.

"A notebook, Conan," Bobster said.

"Your notebook," Simon said.

"Nah, that can't be mine."

"It is. I organized it and took out old papers. I think some of them were from first grade."

We stared. Glass had made a joke.

"I kept the old stuff, in case you wanted it. But I divided the notebook into sections for each subject, and subdivided it into notes, assignments, and completed work. And there's a clip-in dictionary in back and a plastic pouch for note cards, you know, for your research paper."

Simon flipped labeled tabs. "Clean paper here, a

write-on calendar is in front. You can mark due dates for your work." Simon pulled note cards from the pouch. "I separated bib cards from note cards and put them in chronological order. That's the best way to approach your paper." He tucked the cards back into the pouch.

Coop turned the notebook over in his huge hands and looked up at Simon. Coop thrust out his paw, grasped Simon's pudgy one, and shook. "I, you know, uh . . . appreciate it."

Simon colored. "Rob gave me the idea."

Coop looked at Rob, who gave him a thumbs-up. Coop turned back to Glass. "Let's start running tomorrow. Meet me at the track and we'll rev it up."

Simon stammered a yes.

"I'll meet you, too," Rob said.

"No need, Rob," said Coop. "I can handle Simon's exercise program."

"I'll *be* there, Coop."

Coop backed off a step. "No sweat, Rob, I just thought—"

"You're not supposed to think, Coop. Don't forget it."

My stomach clutched. Rob had never said anything like that before, especially to Coop.

Rob held up both hands. "Shit, I'm really sorry. That didn't come out right. I just meant, let me do the thinking, Coop. You have your scholarship to worry about. I don't want to add to your workload."

Rob put his hand on Coop's shoulder. "And you know me," he said. "I have to be in the middle of everything. Why don't you call me an asshole and then forgive me?" He gave Coop his aw-shucks smile.

Coop rubbed his nose and looked around at the rest of us. Then he cleared his throat and said, "You're forgiven." He paused. "Asshole."

"Why don't we hit the road and let Simon get some sleep?" Rob turned back to Glass. "The track at seven."

Simon's eyebrows almost bunched into one again. "In the morning?"

It was after one o'clock when I let myself into the house. As I locked the front door and set the alarm, the door to my father's study opened.

"Young, please come in. I need to speak with you."

My father's voice was soft and easy. But I learned long ago not to trust it. It was a tool he forged to reassure his patients, but there were glass shards and hunks of concrete hidden under its silky surface. I went in.

"Sit down, Young." Dad always smelled of soap and authority. He lowered himself into a tufted leather desk chair that swiveled and rocked. His massive desk was clear of clutter or dust. Tipping back his chair, Dad tapped his chin with a gold fountain pen.

I dropped into a maroon leather club chair. As I sank

into its soft cushions, my father seemed to tower over me.

"Sit up straight, Young. You know you shouldn't slouch."

I hitched up and sat with my back rigid.

"That's better." Dad laid down his pen and cleared his throat. "It seems there's a problem."

I didn't say a word.

"I spoke to Ms. Connally today."

"My counselor?"

"Yes. I called her to see if I could get a printout of class rankings." He retrieved the pen and tapped a staccato beat.

"They don't tabulate those until spring."

"I'm aware of that, Young, but I wanted to see where you stand at this point. See who your competition is."

"Dad, I'm not going to be valedictorian."

"Not with that attitude you're not, nor . . ." He leaned forward. "Nor with your present schedule of classes for next semester."

I lowered my gaze to my clenched hands.

"It seems you've made a few unauthorized changes in your course selections."

Friday, I had gone to Ms. Connally and dropped the second semester of Advanced Bio and signed up for Creative Writing. Traded frogs for fiction. I knew Dad would find out eventually but I didn't think it would be this soon. "Look, Dad, I can explain, I—"

He interrupted, his voice as sharp as his scalpel. "Unless you can explain how writing amateurish fiction can further your progress in your chosen field, I don't want to hear it."

"That's just it!" My voice rose. "It's not my chosen field."

"Young, medicine has been the destiny of every—"

I did the unspeakable. I interrupted my father. "I'm not cut out for it, Dad. I can't even dissect a frog without puking my guts up. I—"

"Lower your voice. And kindly sit down."

I hadn't realized I was standing. I shut my mouth and sat.

"Young, you will go to medical school, you will graduate in the top five of your class, you will drop that writing class and take Advanced Biology, and you will do it Monday at eight o'clock."

I attempted to stare him down but I didn't have the balls. I dropped my eyes again and nodded.

"Good, I'm glad we came to an understanding." His pen tapped against the desk like a heartbeat. "You may go, Young. Get some sleep."

I stood up, walked to the door, and turned to speak.

"Close the door behind you," my father said.

I did what I was told.

I closed the door to my room with care. No slamming doors in this house. My head strummed and my hands fisted and opened, fisted and opened. I paced the room trying to calm down, trying not to scream, trying not to curse my father at the top of my lungs, trying not to cry. I grabbed the fat decorator pillow at the end of my bed and planted my fist deep. The pillow was my father's face, and I smashed his mouth while he told me what to do and how to do it. I pounded the pillow until I cooled out enough to write. A new story with a new ending might help me sleep.

I knew Young wanted to be a writer. He didn't let me read the stuff he wrote in high school and I haven't read his book. That would take me back to a time I don't want to revisit. But Young did a good thing when he assigned his advance and royalties to Coop. And the best part was that Young did it on his own. This time he knew what was right and he did it.

—Ronna Perry

My father never read my short stories. Coop and Bob had both asked, but their interest was more a matter of friendship than literature. I dodged them. But I gave Rob one of my stories the first time he asked.

And he "got" it.

He zoned in on the heart of the story and found the thing I needed the reader to find. So I gave him another one.

Its title was "Touch."

The first lines were:

"His father never touched him. And Mark hungered for it. A hug

with man-smell, cigarettes, aftershave, and sweat. A clap on the back that signaled pride and relationship.

Mark wore that hunger like a bandage, and the young camp counselor pulled the bandage from his wounds, just as he removed the clothes from Mark's body."

Sitting in the blue-and-brown plaid chair in my bedroom, I felt increasingly tense as Rob read the story. When he finished, he didn't look away.

"You're a writer. You'll be a great writer." He arranged the pages, aligning the corners and sides. "There's something else you need to know."

I looked at him. Wanting to know if he understood.

"You're not . . . well, what you think. I can tell from this story that you're confused about it."

My pulse hammered in my ears. "I . . . when it happened . . . I didn't . . . I just let it happen." I looked at Rob. "Doesn't that mean that I'm . . . ?"

There was no revulsion on Rob's face. Nor pity. "You know, when you were a kid your father undressed you and put you in your pajamas? He sat on your bed. If you had a bad dream you might have slept with him. You sat on his lap while he read picture books."

I nodded. My dad was disappointed in me but he hadn't been a monster. He'd done all those things.

"So," Rob continued, "how does a kid know when that stuff turns into something . . . not right?"

"But there was . . . more," I said.

"Maybe. But you listened to a counselor you trusted. And he told you it was right."

I had told myself this stuff, but hearing it from Rob made it real.

"You trusted someone you shouldn't have. That's the only mistake you made."

I lowered my eyes so he wouldn't see the tears of relief and of gratitude.

I wondered if Rob shared secrets with Bob and Coop. Had he found and patched a hole in them as he had in me? He had taken the thing that terrified me and chased it under a rock where it belonged. He was my hero, my savior. My friend.

The phone rang Sunday a little after noon. I answered it in the kitchen as I made a sandwich.

"Young, Coop. C'mon over to Glass's."

"Why?" I cradled the receiver between my ear and shoulder and swiped mayonnaise on the bread.

" 'Cause we want you to see something."

"We?" I licked the knife and tossed it into the sink.

"Me and Glass. I'm over here now."

Coop was at Glass's on his own? I piled on turkey, cheese, pickles, lettuce, and tomato.

"Young, you still there?"

"Yeah," I said, smashing down the top layer of bread.

"See what?"

I took a bite.

"Something slick. Can you get over here?"

"Sure."

"Don't tell Rob you're coming. Okay?"

"Why?"

"You saw him last night. He gets crabbed if we do something with Simon when he's not running the show."

I knew Rob was with Blair today, so it didn't make much dif. But I felt a little guilty somehow. "See you in twenty."

Simon answered his doorbell wearing the navy blue sweats and running shoes bought the day before.

"Come in. Coop's in my study working on the computer."

I'd have sooner believed the sun was shining out of my dick. "He's what?"

I followed Simon. I heard squawks and booms and static-filled explosions along with whines and shrieks and rat-a-tat machine-gun sounds. Over all this, I heard Coop.

"All right! Got another one."

"Way to go, Coop."

"Yea me!"

Turning the corner, I saw Coop hunched over the keyboard of an iMac, pounding buttons, squinting at the screen and shouting.

"What's going on here?" I asked.

"Look at this." Coop pointed to the screen. "Simon says he can help me read better and pass Parks's vocab tests with this thing."

I edged closer and investigated.

"See, it's like a game. Simon says if I learn struc . . . um. . . ." He stuttered to a stop and looked to Glass for help.

"Structural analysis," Simon said.

"Yeah." Coop pounded his forehead with the heel of his hand. "Structural analysis, structural analysis. I can remember that."

I rubbed my eyes. This couldn't be happening. Coop doing schoolwork on a weekend and smiling about it?

"Next thing you'll be walking on the ceiling and playing the piano with your feet," I said.

Coop looked baffled. "Let me show you." He tapped a key and pushed his face closer to the flashing screen. "*Hydro*—that's water. Bam! Fifty points. *Bene*—that means good. Pow! Thirty points. *Spec*—oh, that's hard. Oh, yeah, like in *spectator,* it means to look. Zap! Eighty points. Is this great or what?"

"Young?" Glass motioned to me to join him out in the hall. I left Coop, raised fists over his head in a fit of self-congratulation.

"Glass, I don't know how you did this. We just let him copy our assignments, and sometimes he can't get that straight."

"Maybe that's not doing him any favors."

I shook my head. "Coop wouldn't have gotten past third grade if we didn't."

"Eventually he would."

"Coop's dumb and he knows it."

"Sure." Simon shrugged. "I just wondered who convinced Coop he was dumb, that's all."

I glanced back at Coop pounding the keyboard, having a great time. He never looked that way when he copied our homework.

"Let's get a Coke or something."

I trailed Simon into the kitchen and watched him fill glasses with ice and pull out two cans of Coke. As he poured the Coke, it fizzled and overflowed down the sides of the expensive-looking glass. Simon swabbed the mess, managing to knock over a can. He flushed and turned up his palms. "You fix the Cokes while I get a mop."

I wiped the glasses, poured the drinks, and set them on the glass-and-chrome breakfast room table. I hated those tables: no place to hide your hands.

Simon came back in with a mop and swatted at the puddle. When he finished, he leaned the mop against the wall. As he turned away, it fell, its handle smacking Simon in the back of the head.

He rubbed his head as he sat down. "Story of my life, huh?"

I sipped my Coke, then ran a finger through the beaded condensation ring on the glass.

Coop might have gotten a case of the warm fuzzies for Glass, but I just didn't like the guy. I couldn't put my finger on exactly why.

"Chips?" Glass pulled an oversized door open and grabbed a family-size bag. He held it up. "These all right?"

"Terrific, got any dip?" The voice boomed over my head. Coop's food radar had kicked in. He plucked the package from Glass's hand. "None for you, Glass man. You're going to lose a pound a week, remember?"

Simon grimaced, swiped at his nose, and muttered, "Slave driver."

Coop's grin split his face. "Yo, that's me," he acknowledged as he piled into the chair.

"Can I have my drink?" Simon looked amused and relaxed.

"So, Glass man—do your parents actually live here? Or do they just come by to leave notes on your door? "

"Glass is independently wealthy. He lives here alone, dabbles in stocks and bonds, and goes to high school as a tax dodge." Even I thought I sounded bitchy. Simon definitely had a bad effect on my usual blandness.

Coop made a goofy face. "Guess that was a dumb question, huh?"

"It's the only kind we expect from you," I said. I saw Simon's expression was disapproving and accusatory.

If this little prick thought he could control me with a look, he needed a little sit-down in my father's office chair.

9

Rob was hot and he was cool. You know what I mean? He and Blair were a couple, sure, but nobody ever saw it as a love match. Blair used to be with Lance, then with Rob. She always dated the king because, face it, she's the queen. I like the girl, she's nice as well as pretty. I don't think she led anybody on. So I thought, along with a few other A-list girls, that I could have a shot at Rob. And if being nice to Simon Glass was what it took—fine. It's like Rob went to the pound and picked the ugliest dog there. Because nobody else was going to. After a while, the dog kind of grows on you and you actually think it's sort of cute. You get that, right?

—Caroline Davids

"My parents and I do a good job of staying out of each other's way." Simon sighed. "They're in their study. I should introduce you."

He plodded out of the kitchen, signaling us to follow. We padded across a living room that whispered contemporary cool. He rapped on French doors and pushed in.

"Mom, Dad, this is Young Steward and Jeff Cooper." He flushed and folded his arms across his chest, his hands jammed beneath his armpits.

Glass's parents were a surprise. Mrs. Glass had dark hair like Simon's. She wore it long and pulled back. She was thin, calm, and unruffled, like a Siamese cat.

Perched on a chrome-and-leather desk chair with one foot tucked under her, she tapped a manicured fingernail on the glossy surface of a massive desk and spoke to her husband. "Come out of your fog, dear, and say hello to Simon's friends." Her quicksilver voice blended with the muted music. Verdi.

Simon's dad started, grinned at his wife, and squeezed her hand across the desk. He turned with just a hint of a frown, making parallel creases between his brown eyes. Heavy horn-rim glasses were the only memorable feature on his bland face. "Good afternoon, Simon." He nodded at us. "Boys."

Crisp, clear, no nonsense. Politely acknowledged, but not encouraged to make conversation.

"Young Steward?" Mrs. Glass said. She spoke to her husband. "Would that be Dr. Steward, dear?"

I felt like a piece of furniture.

"Yes, president of the school board, I believe." He glanced at me to get a silent affirmation. "Well," he continued, "your mother and I are working, Simon. You boys have a good afternoon."

Dismissed.

We filed back to the kitchen. Coop rubbed his arms as if he were chilled. Simon settled into his chair. Reaching for the bag, he tore it open and began stuffing potato chips into his mouth. He glanced up at Coop a bit guiltily, then ate more chips. "They're a picture in a magazine, aren't they?"

Coop took the chips. "You know, Glass, my science teacher says you can light one of these things with a match, and there's so much fat in them, it'll burn like a candle."

Coop stuffed the bag into the pantry. "Get some towels, Glass man. We're going to the beach."

"Why?" Simon wheezed.

It caught up with me that Simon wheezed when he was uncomfortable. It was like his father's dismissal had cut off his air supply.

"To play volleyball," Coop said.

"Can't. Too clumsy."

"That was yesterday." Coop flashed his crooked grin. "Things change. Yesterday I didn't know that *hydro* means water." He clopped Simon on the back of the head. "Hustle, Bubba, the beach might move away while we're waiting on you."

Simon shook his head as he scraped back the chair. "Be right back."

After Simon trundled out of the kitchen, Coop

looked at me. "I guess you were right, Young. Glass man does live here alone."

The beach wasn't crowded. It is still plenty hot in September, but the Houston overflow stays in the city after Labor Day, and the locals regain control. We drove the surf line, looking for friendly faces, and ran into Rob. Shirt off, his tanned, muscular body had drawn girls like cat hairs to dark wool. His smile darkened when he saw us with Glass.

"Hey, guys. I called you earlier and couldn't raise a soul. Now I see why." He nodded at Simon. "Good to see you out here, Glass."

Simon blushed and bumbled. The girls looked as if they had just caught a stiff whiff of something dead.

Coop spun the volleyball on the tip of one finger. "Let's get a game up."

"Sure." Rob smiled. "The girls will play, won't you?"

They looked at one another, reluctant, but when Rob put one arm around Blair Crews and whispered in her ear, she smiled and said, "Sure, we'll play, won't we? Caroline, Sherry?" They took another look at Simon and hesitated.

"They'll be on my team," Rob drawled.

That was all it took.

"Lance and Todd are down the beach a ways," Sherry offered. "I'll go get them."

She flounced off, making sure that Rob watched her retreating behind.

"We called Bobster. He said he'd meet us here," I said.

"Great." Rob looked around. "I saw Ronna Perry earlier. Why don't you go look for her while we set up the net, Young?"

"No prob," I said.

"Good," he said. "Come on, ladies, let's plan our team strategy." He leaned close to Caroline.

I drove down the beach and spotted Ronna less than a mile away. Alone, she stretched out in all her long-legged lusciousness on a beach towel, reading. I remembered the day she'd captured my interest. We'd had a speech class together last year. When Mr. Blevins assigned a persuasive speech, Ronna's hand shot up. She told him that a person couldn't be persuaded, only given permission. Blevins countered with the persuasive orations of Adolf Hitler. Ronna argued that Hitler didn't persuade anyone, he simply made it acceptable to unleash the evil already inside. She stunned me. My journal entries became full of her. She entered the world of my short stories.

Now I stopped the car, wiped my sweaty palms against my T-shirt, assumed my I'm-just-too-casual-to-live demeanor, and sauntered over to her. "Mind if I share your towel?" I asked.

Shading her eyes with her hand, she squinted into the sun. "Young?"

"Tis I, m'lady. Your prince has come."

"I have a dog named Prince."

I laughed. "So much for the smooth approach, huh? Bob gave me that line."

"For your information, nobody falls for Bob's lines. His kind of woman goes for his looks."

"I'll make a note of that," I said. "Don't use Bobster's lines unless you are good-looking."

"And Bob's an HSDO."

Ronna laughed at my confusion. "High School Date Only. You believe girls don't categorize guys like you do us?"

Caught. I blushed.

"HSDO, date only in high school where it doesn't count. Not relationship material. Feminine version of arm candy."

Great. More to worry about. Where did I rate on this scale?

She sat up. "Want a Coke?" She reached into a cooler and handed me a wet can.

Sluicing off the water and bits of ice, I pulled the tab and drank. "Thanks."

"You're welcome. What brings a nice guy like you to a place like this all alone?"

My heart was doing drumrolls. Ronna Perry had just called me a nice guy. And all that exposed tanned skin made my mouth water. "Not alone. Scouting expedition. Want to join us for some volleyball?"

"Who's us?"

"Rob, Bobster, Coop, the usual suspects." I paused, then almost whispered, "And Simon."

"Simon? As in Simon Glass?"

"The same. Rob's adopted him, and he's tutoring Coop in English."

"I thought that was your job."

"It was, but my father is pushing me hard to spend more time on my own studies." I wanted to change the subject. "What are you doing out here all alone?"

"Reading."

I took the book from her hand. *The Old Man and the Sea.* "Good place to read it, I guess."

The moment lagged. We listened to the surf.

"English assignment?" I asked.

"Nope, just thought I'd improve my mind."

"'The old man was dreaming about the lions,'" I quoted.

"Huh?"

"That's the last line." I pointed to her book. "Come on." I stood up and pulled Ronna to her feet. "There's a volleyball game a'waitin'."

Ronna gathered her stuff, then followed in her car down the beach. When we got there, the net was going up and Bobster had arrived.

He strolled to my Jeep. "Let's hang back. They don't need us to put up the net."

"Sounds good to me. What took you so long?"

"Dad made me mow the lawn." He laughed. "I don't know why the poor guy never learns."

"You did it again, didn't you?"

"Yup. And it worked again. He almost pushed me into his car to get me away from the mower."

"I don't understand," Ronna said.

Bob grinned. "The Bobster will explaineth. When Dad asks me to mow, I agree without arguing and put the mower deck on the lowest setting. It scalps the grass down to dirt. I mow like crazy right in front of the windows. As soon as my dad sees the bald patches, he runs out and screams that I'm hopeless and he'll never let me touch the mower again." Bobster leaned against the car and took my Coke. "Now is that punishment or what?"

Ronna looked at the crew finishing the net. She pulled her sunglasses off and peered. "Is that Simon? What's happened to him?"

"We shined him up a little."

"A little. He doesn't look so . . . so . . . " She tapered off, searching for the right word. She put her sunglasses back on.

"Come on," Bobster said. "Net's up. Let's play."

Bobster swept off an imaginary cap, bowed low to the ground, and offered his crooked elbow to Ronna. "Lady fair, shall we partake of this game of skill and prowess?"

Ronna curtseyed. "Thank you, kind sir. We shall."

"Right, there's Bobster," Rob shouted. "When the work is done."

"My charm is only exceeded by my timing," Bobster shot back. "I want to serve first."

Boos and hisses boomed out.

Rob organized. "Okay, girls on my team. That makes"— he counted heads—"five. If the big uglies all play together that makes"—he counted again—"six on your team. Girls, that won't be a hardship, will it?"

He grinned at his teammates, hands on hips, eyes twinkling as if they shared a private joke.

"Hey," Lance grumbled. "You mean I gotta play on a team with Glass?"

Simon blushed. "Well, I uh, uh . . ."

Ronna touched Simon's arm. "Don't, Simon. He's a little head." When Simon looked baffled, Ronna shrugged. "As in he thinks with his . . . " She pointed to Lance's crotch. Lance looked to his shorts and we laughed. "Anyway, Rob will handle it."

Rob did. "No, Ansley, you don't have to play with Simon. If you leave, we'll have an even match." Lance puffed up like a blowfish, but he saw the mood was with Glass. He kicked the hot sand.

Rob rescued him. The grin and the teasing tone were back. "But if it's even, that gives the girls and me an easier chance at tromping these poor guys. You don't want that on your conscience, do you?"

"I guess I gotta save all the points Glass is gonna piss away." Lance called Rob "faggot" loud enough to hit its mark, then took his place behind the net.

"Simon, aren't you hot in those heavy sweats? Why don't you take off the shirt?" Malice dusted Caroline's tone.

"If I did"—Simon wheezed—"small children would run shrieking from the beach in horror, and if anyone happened to be equipped with a whaling harpoon . . . " He mimed being shot in the chest. "Wouldn't be pretty." We stared until a giggle trickled out of Caroline's mouth. Soon everyone chuckled. Simon had scored.

I whispered to Rob, "I wouldn't have believed it, but I think you're getting people to like Glass."

Rob nodded, but his eyes narrowed in concentration. "Yeah, but to make him popular, there's something we need." He dug his toes into the sand. "Someone new for class goat." His stare fixed on Lance.

Rob seemed to have a bug up his ass about Lance from day two. I always thought it was connected to Rob's scouring the yearbooks on day one. Lance's picture scattered all over the book told Rob the one person he needed to defeat.

Or maybe Rob didn't need to defeat. Maybe he needed to annihilate.

10

This is not a bad person. This is a person who made bad choices. Do I think he'll make those kinds of choices again? No. Do I think he's a danger to society? No. Do I think he has shown remorse? Let me put it this way. More than one boy died that day. The young man before the parole board is not the young man who stood in the high school equipment room. He has taken responsibility for his actions. He has worked here for five years paying his debt to society. He worked as a teacher, helping inmates learn to read. He's not only rehabilitated himself, he's helped rehabilitate others. Has he forgiven himself for what he did? No. Will he ever? I doubt it. Will he forget what he did? Never.

—Prison Chaplain Joseph Guzman

Glass played volleyball like a cartoon character. On his belly, face in the sand. Every time the ball headed Simon's way, Lance charged from the back, shouldered him aside, and took the play. At first, everybody laughed, but Simon would get up, dust himself off, and thank Lance for rescuing the point. When Rob controlled the ball, he sent it toward Glass. Once, Lance body-blocked Simon so hard he fell into the net and knocked Ronna down with him.

Glass rolled off Ronna, scrambled to his knees, and pulled her to a sitting position. "Are you okay?"

"I'm fine, Simon."

Rob stepped up. "Lance, quit hogging the ball and pounding Glass into the sand."

"Yeah, Lance. Go prove your manhood someplace else," Ronna said, flicking grit off her pert ass.

Blair and Caroline agreed in low murmurs.

"I've had enough of this crap. Come on, Todd. Let's find some real action."

Todd looked around, unsure.

"I'll be glad to give you a ride home if you want to stay," Rob offered.

Todd picked up the volleyball. "Thanks, I think I'll hang around awhile."

I think Lance had adjusted to the drop from king to B-lister. But now his friends were turning on him. Lance spun on his heel and stomped to his car. He left, spraying sand.

"What a jackass," Blair Crews complained, brushing sand out of her hair.

"Forget him," Rob said. "Let's plaaaaaay ball."

*   *   *

Monday morning Simon made his first appearance as a human being for the school population. He wore jeans, Top-Siders, and a striped rugby jersey. His hair shone and lay flat on his head, the front flapping over his wary eyes. Beach time had swabbed color on his previously pasty cheeks. As they wound through the tables, Rob engaged him in conversation.

The rabble stared and whispered. They goggled when Coop hailed them. "Rob, Glass man, over here."

Blair and Caroline waved and Sherry gave Simon a mock swat on the arm. "Hey, Simon. Recovered from that game?"

Lance swaggered up. "Yeah, Glass, I'll bet you have bruises all over your fat butt. I knocked you in the sand at least eight times." He hooked his thumbs in his belt loops.

"Eight?" Simon asked. "It feels like more than that." He clapped Lance on the shoulder. "You might have busted my butt, Lance, but you saved all those points for me."

The faces in the crowd were both shocked and bewildered even as they laughed. What was this? Simon Glass making Lance Ansley look like an ass?

As Rob turned to Simon, the bell rang. "See you at lunch, Glass?"

"Sure. I'll save a table."

We ambled toward our classrooms. "Nice work, Rob."

"Ain't it so?" Rob said. "Glass thinks you don't like him."

"So, maybe I don't. Is it required?"

Rob wasn't smiling now. "Let's just say it would be advantageous."

I swallowed hard and was silent.

"Hey," Rob said. "Just fix your dislike onto someone that deserves it more."

"And that would be . . ."

"Lance."

When we got to the cafeteria, Glass was pulling things from his paper bag.

Rob grabbed the sack. "What are you doing?"

Simon looked surprised and guilty. He swiped his nose.

"Don't do that," Rob said.

"What?"

"Wipe your nose."

"Okay." Simon reached up, about to rub his nose again, then stopped. "I guess I do that when I'm nervous."

"You must be nervous all the time," Bobster said. "Let's get some food. I'm hungry."

"Me, too," Coop said.

"Ditch the McDweeb Meal and come with us," Rob commanded.

We pushed through the crowd and got in line.

"Simon, you get salad, no dressing, and milk." Coop pointed to a green substance. "That's salad."

"You sure?" Glass asked.

"Great, the young princes have a comedian with them," the cafeteria lady snarled.

"What's on the menu today?" Rob asked.

"Soup," the worker said. "What's it look like?"

"Don't answer that question," Simon said. "You could be held criminally liable."

"For what?" Rob asked.

"Assault with a dead weapon." Simon sniffed at the soup.

"Not bad, Glass," Rob acknowledged, looking to the cafeteria lady. "What's in it?"

"Oh, there's the Band-Aid I lost," she muttered, stirring the soup and peering into the pot. "Here you go." She slopped the soup into a bowl and handed it to Rob. "You get the Band-Aid for free."

Rob raised his palms in defense. "I'll just have salad, too."

We found a table. Blair Crews, Todd, Caroline, and Sherry joined us. People still looked at Simon with questions in their eyes, but conversations continued. In only one day, Rob had managed to get Simon tolerated, if not completely accepted.

When the others left the table, Rob talked strategy. "You know, Simon. There's more we have to do."

"What do you mean?" Coop asked.

"Here." Bobster pushed his extra milk over to Coop.

"Rob's right. Just because nobody's launching snot rockets at you doesn't make you popular."

"So, how do I do that?" Simon shrugged. "Pay them? Nobody has that much money."

"You know, Glass. I think that's it," Rob said. He tapped his fingers on the tabletop in a rapid tattoo.

"What's *it*?" I asked. "Paying them?"

"No, Glass is right, nobody has that much money. But he does have a quick wit. That's our play."

"Play?" Coop was bewildered.

"Sure, Young's popular because he's rich, Bobster's got chick appeal, and Coop is our gridiron hero. We need something for Simon. You heard the Wicked Witch of the Lunch Line. She thought he was a comedian."

"I don't think you can pull it off. But plan without me." I stood. "I have to go see Ms. Connally."

"Didn't you change your schedule Friday?" Rob asked.

"I did. I'm changing it back."

Rob's voice was gentle. "Because you want to or because your dad told you to?"

"It's a health thing. I have to change back in order to keep my head attached to my body."

After school, we met in the weight room. Coop held Simon's feet and counted sit-ups. Simon was red-faced and sweating. "Ten, eleven, twelve, c'mon, Simon, you're doing great. Keep going."

"How many do I have to do?" Simon panted.

"Until I tell you to stop. Let's go. Fifteen, sixteen."

"Young, can you take Simon home?" Rob leaned on the handles of the rowing machine.

"I guess."

"Good, I have something to do, and Coop has football practice."

"Glass, why don't you have a car?" Bobster asked. "Your family's loaded."

"I don't have my license."

We sucked air.

"I told you, Rob," Bobster said. "This guy is hopeless."

"My parents always work late. Nobody ever taught me to drive."

"So what about Driver's Ed.?"

"Nobody to take me."

Bob broke the silence. "If that doesn't . . .' He paused, searching. "Chew the gopher!"

Another entry for *The Book of Bob*. Destined to be a classic. Even Simon laughed.

"Bobster," Rob said. "Teach the Glass man to drive."

"I don't know . . ."

"You're the only one man enough for the job," Rob said.

Simon sat up and wiped his face with his shirttail. "I don't know, either. Do you have lots of insurance, Bobster?" He paused. "Or a death wish?"

"I'll teach you to drive. But if we have a wreck, at least get me killed in a way that has no visible facial injuries. I want to leave a gorgeous corpse."

I took Bobster and Simon home. Bobster stretched out in the backseat, popped sunflower seeds into his mouth, and spit the hulls out the window.

"You know, Glass, you did good with Lance today, but this witty stuff is only going to take you so far. Sooner or later you'll have to do something."

"Like?"

He popped a right jab into the air. "Punch him out."

I groaned. "Get real, Bob."

"He can't play defense all his life. Simon needs to be like the Bobster. Use his fists. Prove he's got some balls."

"Bobster's right," Simon said.

Bob hadn't had a fight since fifth grade. He'd just been talking about it ever since he'd sucker-punched a mean and skinny STP—*Book of Bob* for "trailer-park trash." More correctly, "Squirrels in Trailer Parks." Useful only to clean engines.

We pulled into Bob's driveway. "Of course I'm right. The Bobster's the *man*." He slid out of the car. "Glass, driving lesson tomorrow afternoon."

We headed toward Glass's house.

"Rob told me about your Creative Writing course."

"That's my ex-Creative Writing course." I clenched

my teeth. It was like I had traded places with Simon. Rob was talking about poor, pitiful Young with this geek. "And why did he tell you about that?"

"Don't get mad. He told me because he thinks you're a terrific writer, and I could help."

"Nobody's going to change my dad's mind."

"I'm not going to try. There's another way."

I was a little intrigued. "Okay, I'll bite; what can you do?"

"Computer hacking." Simon rustled around, placing his back to the car door to face me. "Every teacher has a computer in the classroom. They send in absences and final grades to the main program. The office uses that program to print report cards."

"I know all this."

"I'll hack into the main program. You'll be taking Creative Writing, but the report card that goes to your dad will read "Advanced Biology." I'll build in an override, so that when your Creative Writing teacher enters your grade, the main program picks it up as Biology."

I thought a minute. Wondering how this could go wrong. "What if my dad calls?"

"Everything in the office reads 'Biology.' It can only go wrong if he looks for you in the biology classroom. Does he come to the school often?"

About as often as a total eclipse. "Glass," I said. "It might work."

He leaned back into the seat. "I'll need to find the

way into the program. That's not hard. After that I enter the school files from home."

The thought ghosted through my mind that Glass was more than book smart. He was devious.

I wheeled onto his street. "Does it work on absences?"

"Sure. Why?" Simon asked.

I turned into his driveway. Rob would love this. I could make nice to Simon and make not-nice with Lance. "Because I can think of a way for you to take the offensive with Lance."

Simon looked puzzled, and then a smile spread over his face. "You mean—"

"We could have him trying to explain away unexcused absences until he doesn't know whether to scratch his ass or lick his lips."

Simon squinted and rubbed his hands together. "This is going to be fun."

11

When I heard what happened, it shocked me. But when
I heard who was involved, I doubted my own sanity. I
know that Rob oozed animal magnetism and charm and
you might not want to trust charmers. In teaching, you
meet lots of those, but Young Steward? Yes, in person
he *was* kind of "buttoned up." Repressed anger, I guess,
looking at it from hindsight. Not hard to understand if
you've had a conversation with his father. But his English
teacher showed me Young's writing. It was observant
and sensitive. How could he have gotten swept up in
this? I went to Huntsville once and visited. I could never
go again. It broke my heart to see him there.

—Janice Connally, BrazosVale
high school counselor

The next morning I found Simon. "How do we work this
schedule business?"

"First, you change your schedule back to Creative
Writing."

"Connally's gonna have a shit-fit."

"You have to be registered in the course before I build in the override."

"Okay, I'll do that now. What's next?"

"I go to the office and find the code to the main program."

"And you'll do that, how?"

Simon looked amused. "All it takes is someone clumsy."

"When?"

"I can get the code today, but we need to wait a couple of weeks before I hack the program. Give everyone a chance to forget anything unusual. Your Creative Writing class isn't until next semester, right?"

"What about Lance?"

"That'll have to keep." Simon looked around. "I'll go with you to Connally's office and get the access code now."

When Glass and I walked in, Ms. Connally looked perplexed. "What can I do for you boys?"

"Nothing for me, Ms. Connally, I just came along with Young." Simon was in his bumbling mode. "Don't mind me." He pulled his backpack in front and tugged on the zipper. "This thing always gets stuck," he said, yanking.

"I want to drop Advanced Bio and sign up for Creative Writing again."

Connally sighed, rolled her head back, and massaged the nape of her neck. I heard little cricking noises as she rocked her head back and forth. "Young, how many times do we have to go through this?"

"I know, Ms. Connally, but I finally talked my dad into it. I promised him I would take Bio at the community college. It gives me dual credit for high school and college, doesn't it?" I oozed juvenile sincerity.

"Yes, it does. And it's a good idea. But it doesn't count toward your class ranking. Does your father understand that?"

"Yes, ma'am, he does."

"I'll make the change." She turned to her computer, gave a calculating glance, and tapped the keys.

Simon worked on the recalcitrant zipper. He edged closer to the desk and yanked hard. The zipper flew open; books cascaded out and landed on Ms. Connally's keyboard. "Oh, gosh! I'm sorry. Here, let me help." Simon scattered the books, then tripped and fell across the screen and Ms. Connally.

The counselor pushed back. Simon clambered up.

"Oh, sorry." While his body blocked her view of the screen, Simon punched a key. The screen went blank.

"Look what I've done." Simon grabbed his books and pointed to the screen. "I lost your whole program."

Ms. Connally shook her head. "Don't worry, Simon. The program saves itself when it shuts down."

As she pecked the keys, Simon was at her elbow, stuffing books back into his backpack. His eyes watched her fingers; then a slow smile tugged his mouth. "I'll wait outside for you, Young. Before I do any more damage." He bumbled his way out.

"All right, we've got you signed up." She hit the print command, ripped off a schedule change, and tossed it to me. "Get that signed and you'll be in business." She smiled. "I'm glad your father agreed, Young. Your English teacher says you have talent."

I hurried out, grabbed Simon by the elbow, and pulled him around the corner. "That was unbelievable, Glass."

"Do you think she suspected?"

"No way. She was just glad to get you out of her office before you destroyed the furniture."

Glass shrugged. "People wanting to get rid of me is something I'm used to."

"Well, it worked to your benefit this time."

Simon slid a sideways look at me. He was cool and relaxed. "No, Young, it worked to *your* benefit."

My good feeling vanished. "I owe you one," I muttered.

I wanted to smash Glass's face. When Rob helped me out, it was like he was supporting me. But when Simon did—he rubbed my nose in it.

12

I filed a suit against the school district. If they had even the most rudimentary of security systems for the database, this wouldn't have gotten so out of hand.

—James Glass

That afternoon Bob gave Simon his first driving lesson. No one offered his car as sacrifice, so Simon learned to crank and cruise in Brown Dog. Brown Dog was a pickup truck that Bobster's dad had bought for one hundred dollars. Its previous owner was a shrimper, and it was held together with rust and homemade resin. It smelled of seriously dead fish.

The next morning, Glass was dressed and combed into acceptable standards, but he looked like crap. He had dark shadows under his eyes, and he handed Bob a check.

"Here, Bob, this should cover the damage."

Bobster fingered the check and explained, "Simon murdered my mailbox." He sighed. "And the Dog didn't even get a dent."

"I told you I couldn't drive," Simon said.

"Don't worry, we'll have you driving before you know it. We'll try another lesson Thursday."

"Let's give up."

"Give what up?" Rob appeared, clapping one hand on Glass's shoulder.

"Driving lessons," Simon blurted.

Rob stared at each of us. "Who says?"

"Me," Simon said. "I demolished Bobster's mailbox. It was DOA, no chance of resuscitation."

"No problem. You'll get better," Rob said.

"But I might kill a person rather than a mailbox. Let's forget it."

"Not an option. You *will* get your license because Bob will teach you to drive." Rob strode away.

"What's with Rob?" Coop asked, joining us.

"Hitler complex," Simon muttered.

Coop shrugged. "Hey, Simon, can you check these discussion questions we had for English?"

"Coop did his homework? By himself?" Bobster was shell-shocked. "Did the sun come up in the west?" He started to follow Coop and Simon but spied Ginger Donalson. "Darlin,' are you following me?" He tagged behind her.

I looked around, then trudged up the steps alone.

*   *   *

Days followed one another, and September changed into October. We changed short sleeves for long sleeves, but the biggest change was that people got used to Simon Glass. Bobster worked on Simon to quit spitting when he talked. Even I had to admit that Glass was shaping up.

Though our team was in the dumper, Coop was having a great season as star linebacker. No offers had been made, but the scouts were watching, and Coop gave them a show.

Rob came up with an idea that worked big. He talked Glass into getting a team-mascot costume of a snarling wolverine. We petitioned the principal to allow Simon on the track with the cheerleaders. Deputy Dog, our hallowed leader, approved, and Simon was bouncing and cheering on Friday nights. We kept the mascot's identity a secret from everyone, even the cheerleaders, and the school buzzed with the mystery. With a school the size of B'Vale, the process of elimination was nearly impossible, and we made it harder by having different contenders be conspic-uously absent at some games and paying a junior high kid to wear the uniform until halftime at one game while Simon sat in the stands.

The driving lessons continued until Bob pronounced Simon ready to take his driving test. They made an appointment for him to take it in a week.

And Simon said the time was right for his hacker magic. We slouched in the chairs at our usual table in the Commons.

"Young, I'm going to get into the program tonight and change your schedule. You want to come over and see how I do it?"

"I don't know, I have to—"

"Let's watch. Maybe we can sneak a look into Lance's file and find out some dirt." Bobster was still pushing Simon to take the offensive.

"Yeah," Coop added.

"Where's Rob?" I asked.

"Dinner with Blair's parents," Bob said.

"All right, I'll pick y'all up at seven," I said.

Simon answered the door and led us down the hall. We slumped in his study while he sat at the computer. "This isn't complicated, but I doubt you want to memorize the process, right?"

"Tell Coop elves do it, and he'll be fine," Bobster said.

"Hey, man, you don't know they don't," Coop shot back.

Simon clicked and clacked at the keyboard. "Here we go. It was easier than I thought. A lot of schools have a protection program." He clicked more. "I have here the file of Steward, Thaddeus Richard, IV."

I looked over Glass's shoulder. "Yup, that's my file. Get on with it."

"Thaddeus Richard! My man!" Bob shouted.

Simon typed. "Here's next semester's schedule. You're registered for Creative Writing." He tapped and plunked. "Let's see if it worked." Simon pulled out of the program, then reentered. "I'll pull up the teacher's file." He did, and my schedule with Creative Writing appeared on the screen. "And we enter a grade." Simon tapped in an eighty-two.

"Gimme a break, Glass. I want a ninety-two."

"This is just a trial run. The grade won't stay."

"It's the principle."

He brushed his hair off his forehead and sighed. "Fine, I'll change it. I'll send in. Then we'll check the main file and see what we came up with." His fingers flew and the computer changed screens. My schedule appeared again. This time it read "Advanced Biology" and in the grade column was a ninety-two.

Coop hunkered at my elbow. "That's as slick as grease through a goose."

I put my hand on Coop's face and pushed him back. "Thank you for that analogy."

Bobster appeared in Coop's place. "Glass, could we change our grades? You know old ones. I have a D in—"

Glass removed his hands from the keyboard. "That's how hackers get caught. Something as important as a final grade that's been on the record. It's remembered. Your English teacher, the next year's English teacher who brags about how she was a better teacher because you made a B when you had her. Your parents. Your counselor."

Bob deflated. "Shit a donkey. Well, let's get to Lance's file."

Simon looked relieved and hunched over the keyboard.

"Look at this. Ansley's medical file says he's allergic to strawberries. Says he breaks out in hives," Bobster said.

"So what, we're going to put in some absences, not feed him," Coop said.

"We could use that information someday," Simon said. He tapped his fingers against the desktop, seemingly lost in thought. He shrugged. "Whatever, I'm going to put in one absence for last week."

A shrewd look crossed Bob's face. He asked, "If we can put in absences, can we take them out?"

"Sure."

"Well, I already have two, why don't we ditch them?"

Simon looked hesitant. "I don't know. That's illegal. I mean, Lance will get his absences straightened out, but changing yours is messing with records that are audited by the state."

"Big deal, you're changing Young's schedule."

"That seems like semantics. He's still taking a class, and he's working for the grade," Simon said.

"Do it," I said. "Don't worry so much about the rules."

"You should talk," Bobster said.

"What's that mean?"

"Chill, Young. Bobster's just goofin' on you. Whadda ya say, Simon, why don't you fix Bobster up?" Coop turned his spaniel eyes on Glass.

Simon shrugged. "It's not such a big deal, I guess." He tapped. "You're fixed up. Absence-free."

"Rob was with me both days. Dump his, too."

"Why not? I've come this far. But that's it. I'm not crawling the file of every person you know. The more time we spend in here, the better the chance of getting pegged." Simon accessed Rob's file. We dropped back onto the sofa. Coop got hunger pangs and wanted to order pizza.

"This is strange." Simon turned around. "I pulled up Rob's file and . . . " He trailed off, turned and looked at the computer screen again. "It looks like Rob isn't who he says."

"What? Rob isn't who he says he is?" Bob asked.

"When I typed in 'Rob Haynes,' his file came up. But look here." Simon pointed to the top line. "It says 'Haynes, Robert.' But here's an asterisk. When you look down here, it says 'Baddeck, Robert Haynes, Junior.' Then in parentheses it says that 'Haynes' is not his legal name. That means that Rob is really Rob Baddeck. Do you guys know anything about that?"

We looked at one another. No, nobody knew.

"I don't get it," Coop said. "Why wouldn't Rob use his real name?"

"Maybe he's a spy," Bobster offered.

Nobody bothered to answer.

"Are his parents divorced?" Simon asked.

We looked at one another again.

Bob picked it up. "I don't know, Glass. He never said. I assumed his dad was dead or something. He never goes off on weekend duty visits."

"What do you know about Rob?" Simon asked me.

I shrugged. "Not much. He transferred in last year before Thanksgiving."

Simon pointed to the screen again. "This gives his entry date as November third."

"Yeah," Bobster said. "I remember he said somewhere out of state, but he never did say exactly where."

"Yeah," Coop said. "I asked him where out of state, and he said it was a Podunk town no one's ever heard of."

"The file says he came from Foley, Texas."

"By Clear Lake? That's just down the road. That's Podunk but not out of state," Coop said.

"No kidding, Sherlock," I said with a growing sense of betrayal. Why hadn't Rob told me this stuff?

"You don't need to pick on Coop," Simon said.

"Bite me, Glass. Just run the computer."

Simon's mouth slid into a hard line. "Fine, I guess I should remember my place from now on." He clattered the keys and the printer started whirring. "I'll make a printout so we don't have to stand here all day."

I mentally shot Glass the bird. It pissed me off whenever he showed some spine.

We studied the hard copy. It showed Rob was indeed a transfer from the Clear Lake district, his mother was Baddeck, Louise, and his father was Baddeck, Robert H. It showed Rob's address correctly and listed his father as living in Foley. There was something else strange. The file said Rob's mother worked at Dow as a secretary, but showed his father formerly being an engineer at one of those companies that contract most of their work to NASA. The record did not reveal a present place of business.

"Maybe his dad was a spy." It seemed the idea of international intrigue appealed to Bob. All those James Bond movies must have warped him.

"Why don't any of you guys know this stuff about Rob?" Glass asked.

"Rob. . . " Bob looked at me. "He never talks about himself."

We were quiet and in a pondering mode when I said, "He manages to get us to do all the talking."

"Maybe his parents had a real bad divorce, and he doesn't want to use his dad's name or visit him," Coop offered. "We don't have to make this some kind of big deal, you know."

"That's probably it," Simon said. "Let's forget it. I'll change his absences and get out of his file. Rob'll tell us when and if he wants to. Right?"

"Right," Bobster said.

"Yo," Coop agreed.

I hesitated a minute. Simon turned and gave me his hard-eyed stare.

"Sure," I said. "Why not?"

13

I thought what those boys were doing for Simon, sort of adopting him into their group, was such a hopeful thing. In my experience, high school cliques are more about excluding people. When Rob came to me with his plan, I thought it was generous. I also thought it would be fun. And mostly I thought that the other students would learn something about the goodness of people from it. They learned something about people. But nothing about goodness.

I retired from education that year. I sell insurance now.

—Charles Crocker, former principal
of BrazosVale High School

Our last football game, the first week of November, was Homecoming. Rob thought the time was right for a major push to make Simon Mr. Popularity.

"How do you plan to make that miracle happen?" Bobster asked.

"I haf my vays," Rob said in a mock-Gestapo voice.

"In fact, I'm on my way to see Deputy Dog to put the plan into action."

"You're gonna get the principal to *make* people like Simon?" Coop asked. "I don't think it'll work."

"Rest, Coop. Save up those thinking cells for the ACT." I patted Coop on the back. The ACT test was the Saturday after Homecoming. Coop had to score a meager eighteen to get in line for an athletic scholarship. For Coop, this would be a struggle.

"Yeah, I oughta rest up my brain, huh?"

"This is how it's gonna work." Rob leaned in close and told us the plan.

"Not bad, Rob. Not bad at all," I said.

"Might work," Bobster agreed.

"Yo," Coop added.

"Oh, no. Do I have to?" Glass moaned. He covered his head with his arms.

Rob picked up one elbow and pried open one of Simon's tightly closed eyes. "Yes, you do," Rob said, nodding emphatically. "You most certainly do." He dropped Simon's eyelid.

"Oh, no," Glass said again.

"Off to get the okay from Deputy Dog." Rob glided away.

The Deputy gave his approval. In fact, he thought it was a terrific idea. Bobster was put in charge of choreography, I was to head up publicity, Coop was to keep it a secret and concentrate on winning the football game, and Rob was to coordinate everything. The time wasn't right for Simon to have a date; it would interfere with the plans. So, that was one hurdle we didn't have to jump. It was, however, a hurdle I had yet to leap.

Bob made his move on Ginger Donalson. I think his former girlfriend was drinking Clorox under his bedroom window in protest. Rob would be escorting Blair Crews, our head cheerleader and winner of every popularity contest since kindergarten. She was a shoo-in for Homecoming Queen, which would make Rob Homecoming Beau.

Rob and I were alone in the weight room that afternoon. I counted and huffed out sit-ups on the slant board as Rob pedaled the stationary bike. Neither of us spoke.

Finally, "Steward, when are you gonna get a date for Homecoming? The boat is about to sail, my man."

"I was thinking of skipping the festivities, Rob."

"Why?"

I felt the room turn chilly.

"Got lots to do. Busy, busy, busy," I said. "I've got the underwear drawer to straighten out, old copies of *TV Guide* to catch up on."

"Cut the bullshit, Young. You're going to Homecoming."

It was a command.

"Why is this so important to you?"

"Because we're going to turn the tide with Simon at the dance. We all have to be there."

"He doesn't need me. Coop practically wags his tail when Glass is around, and you're running the show. I can take a pass on seeing Simon's triumph."

"It pisses you off that you're not Coop's one-and-only hero anymore, doesn't it?"

"Save the amateur analysis for someone who gives a rat's ass."

As Rob pumped the pedals, the wheel made a ticking sound. I kept counting. My abs screamed, but somehow the pain comforted me. I kept counting.

"I know what the problem is, Young."

I kept counting.

"You want to ask Ronna Perry, but you're waiting for something."

"What am I waiting for, Great One?" I stopped to catch my breath.

"I don't know. A sign from the gods. The stars to align. Someone to tell you to do it."

I'm not sure why I didn't answer. I started my sit-ups again.

"Go ahead. Ask her."

I lost count. I rolled off the board and snapped up a towel. "I'm gonna bail."

Rob nodded and kept pumping the pedals.

*　　*　　*

"Homecoming under the Stars." That was the theme of the big do. I guess the planning committee found posters from the zillion other years that Homecoming was under the stars.

Ronna and I walked into the dimly lit gym that was laced by spotlights pointing up to the ceiling, the light flickering and dancing among foil-covered stars that quivered at the end of fishing line. An antique mirrored ball that had been used at every Homecoming since 1965 rotated and flashed in the center. We had finally won a football game, and everyone was pumped. Even the ratty stars and the tacky mirrored ball threw off their own brand of magic, and the place held a slightly frayed enchantment.

Ronna was definitely princess material. Her dark hair framed eyes the color of champagne. Ron was long and lean and walked with a straight-backed ease. She made my blood pound.

"I can't wait to see what's going on. Those posters are great," Ronna said as we entered the double doors.

She referred to the posters that had lined the halls for two weeks. WHO IS THE WOLVERINE? and HOMECOMING SURPRISE—DON'T MISS IT! and THE WOLVERINE UNMASKED! The rabble had been buzzing with their guesses and suppositions. There were betting pools with the odds rising and falling as rumor changed and armchair detectives announced their deductions.

Rob was on top of the world. His usual roost. In a navy blazer and striped tie, he exuded the aura of a movie star.

"Young, let's dance." The lights reflected in Ronna's eyes. Her short hair made the back of her head seem so vulnerable that I yearned to cup my hand against the soft curve where skull rounds into neck.

Instead, I shrugged. "Sure, that's what we're here for."

She wrinkled her nose, animating the freckles, and drifted into my arms like an indrawn breath. "You waited a long time to ask me to this dance."

"I'm sorry," I murmured into her scented hair.

"I was worried, waiting for you to make a move."

"It's a brand-new century; why didn't you ask me?" I said.

She held up her hand and wiggled her fingers. "What do you see?"

Her nails were chewed to the quick.

"Those," she said, "are evidence that my self-confidence is mostly a fraud." She grinned. "I thought I'd end up being the only princess without a date." She pulled back and squinted through her lashes at me. "Well? No comment?"

I drew her back against me. "Is that true?"

"Would I lie? What would I have to gain?"

That one stumped me for a minute. "I guess to flatter me. Make me like you."

"But you already do."

I laughed outright. "Are you sure about the confidence being a fraud?"

"I have self-doubt, but I'm not stupid. You do *so* like me." She walked her bitten fingertips across my shoulder, then yanked my earlobe. "Don't you? You'd better say so or you'll be missing an ear very soon."

She snugged her face against my neck. I smoothed my fingers over her hair and rounded my palm at the base of her head.

"Yes, I do like you, a lot." I paused a minute, feeling her breath against my throat and her breasts against my chest. "But you can have the ear anyway. Consider it a party favor."

She giggled. "I could make a necklace."

"Too grisly—press it in a book, like a flower."

She leaned back, mischief making her eyes sparkle. "Tell you what, you keep it for me, but it's mine. Nobody else gets to touch it." She kissed her index finger and touched it to my ear. "There. You're branded. I own that ear."

Rob appeared next to us, cleared his throat, and bowed in imitation of a discreet English butler.

The stars dulled.

"What do you need, Rob?"

"You, *compadre*. Ronna, can I have a word with the Steward? I'll just be a minute."

Ronna sighed dramatically. "Well, at least the ear is mine." She grinned. "I have to go anyway. They're about to announce the Homecoming Queen, and I have to put on that stupid ribbon."

I watched her sail away.

"Talk to the journalism drudge and make sure he is where he can get good pictures of Glass."

"I already took care of it," I said.

"I know I'm being a pain."

"In the butt," I added.

"Yep, I know, but I need this to go perfect."

I wondered for the hundredth time why this was so necessary to Rob. The only thing I could find was that he needed control the way I needed approval.

He slapped me lightly on the back. "You're the only one I can count on."

I talked to the journalism drone again. He gave me a bored look and assured me that he'd do his job. Ms. Connally and the cheerleading sponsor lined the girls' escorts along one of the white stripes on the floor. The girls stood opposite us, fussing with their banners and whispering to one another frantically. I took my place. Next to Lance.

He leaned close. "Hey, asshole, only reason you're here with Ronna is I waited too late to ask her." He smirked at me. "Had to give Blair the boot. A senior chick is too old." I looked around. His date was a sophomore. "Get 'em young and train 'em right, " Lance said.

My hands clenched into fists.

The lead singer tapped on the microphone. "Okay, boys and girls, and even you folks that haven't decided which you are. Close your mouths and breathe through your noses. Your hallowed leader is gonna come up here and present the best flesh on the hoof in your fair school. Here he is, kiddies, DEP-YOU-TEE DAAAAAWWG!"

He drawled the "dog" as he spun, and gestured with an outstretched hand as he bowed. Only his middle finger was extended.

"Thanks, Alex," Deputy said. "We'll be sure that picture doesn't make the yearbook. Now, let's see who will be our Homecoming Queen." He pulled a piece of paper from his pocket. "From the sophomore class, our princesses are: Sandy Krenshaw, escorted by Junior Beau, David Wills."

Suddenly a trumpet player in the band stood and a *Ta ta ta dah* blared. One of the spotlights swiveled its aim from the ceiling to the double doors at one end of the gym. The drummer began a tattoo, rolling it louder and louder, crashing to a thunderous finale as the gym doors burst open to reveal the Wolverine mascot, complete with the Homecoming Queen's rhinestone tiara cocked on his oversized head.

The Wolverine twirled on one heel, then began a hip-hopping dance from pool of light to pool of light, in a path to the center of the gym. He whirled and bowed to clamorous applause.

Strutting to the line of awaiting princesses, he bowed to Sandy, took her in his arms, and waltzed her to the stage. Depositing Sandy, the Wolverine dropped to one knee, bent his huge muzzle, kissed her hand, popped up, and sashayed merrily back to the princesses, where he began the giddy ritual again.

When all the girls were whirled to the dais, Deputy waited for the applause to die down. "The moment is at hand. The Wolverine will present the crown to this year's Homecoming Queen. Since the results are secret, I'll tell the mascot the name of our winner."

Jazzing his way to the front, the Wolverine leaned forward, one paw cupped around his huge pointed ear. When the Deputy whispered, the mascot raised his furry arms above his head and clapped, pulled the crown from his head, and carried it in front of him like a fragile egg. He stood before each Queen candidate and offered the crown, then snatched it away, shaking his head with extreme regret. He did this to every girl, faced the crowd, and gave a hopeless shrug. Back at the microphone, he gestured for the Dog to whisper again.

The Wolverine nodded and wandered along the stage behind the waiting girls and plunked the tiara on Blair Crews's head.

The crowd applauded and Rob bent to give Blair the customary kiss. The Wolverine jumped between them, whipped off the big fake head, tossed it aside, grabbed

Blair, leaned her back in a movie-star pose, and planted a kiss on her surprised mouth.

Applause, gasps, cheers, drumbeats, trumpet flourishes, and piercing whistles shook the gym.

Simon pulled Blair upright. Both blushed crimson. Simon appeared abashed and embarrassed now that the mask was off. Blair adjusted her crown, grabbed Simon, bent him back as he had done her, and kissed him soundly. He stretched out one leg and pointed his furry toes.

The roar measured at least a six on the Richter scale. The band cranked up, and Deputy shouted into the microphone. "And now our Homecoming Queen, Miss Blair Crews, will dance with the Homecoming Beau, Rob Haynes."

The music pumped up. Rob leaned over to Blair and spoke. She nodded and Rob gestured to Simon, signaling that he should dance with the new queen. Blushing furiously, Glass kissed Blair's hand. Taking her into his arms, he danced her to the center of the gym under the shimmering ball of light.

Glass was dancing with a queen under a spotlight and the crowd approved. It was magic all right. Pure magic.

14

Simon Glass was amazing at Homecoming. We'd been just kind of being nice to Simon because of Rob and, face it, he was getting more presentable every day. But Homecoming—he came into his own. He didn't hang onto Rob's coattails, he took over, got confidence or pride, or . . . something. It was the greatest night. No bad endings. Everybody was happy.

—Ginger Donalson

As the evening progressed, Simon danced with all the Homecoming nominees. Now that he was Simon Glass rather than the Wolverine, he bumbled and fumbled, but none of the girls seemed to mind. Glass had become the greatest thing since chocolate.

"Would you look at him?" Bobster groaned. "I busted my hump teaching him my best moves and look at him. He dances like his toes are stapled together."

"He looked great before," Coop said.

"Go figure," Bobster sighed. "But it worked, didn't it? Glass is the belle of the ball."

It was true. Simon was congratulated, backslapped, and hand-shook as a conquering hero. He nodded and blushed and grinned his thanks, then bumbled his way over to us.

"Yo! Glass, you the *man!*" Coop shouted.

"Thanks, Coop. Hey, you guys. Is this something else?"

"Do I get my dance now, Simon?" Ronna asked.

I started to say something, anything, but Rob elbowed in. "Yeah, Glass, you haven't danced with this princess yet."

"I thought I'd leave one uncrippled," Simon said.

"Oh, no, you don't. A princess is royalty, and you can't refuse." Rob took Ronna's hand and placed it on Glass's elbow. She curtseyed and guided him out to the middle of the floor. Placing her hand delicately on his shoulder, standing at arm's length, she nodded gravely while she slid her other hand into his. They moved to the music, but Simon's Wolverine tail tangled between their feet. Ronna grabbed the end and held it, occasionally tickling him under the chin with its tip.

Feeling like I'd swallowed fish bones, I watched them dance. Ronna laughed delightedly when Simon trod on her toes, and he gazed down into her upturned face, chatting and smiling and obviously smitten.

When she returned, Ronna was exuberant. "Simon is having the time of his life."

"So I see."

She poked me with her finger. "Don't be that way, Young. Simon thinks the world of you."

"Lucky me."

"Grrr," she growled. "Such a grizzly old bear you are. Let Simon have his night."

"He can have as many nights as he wants, as long as he gets his own girlfriend."

"The world has gone cuckoo," Ronna said. "Six weeks ago Lance Ansley was popping the elastic on the school whipping boy, and now Young Steward is jealous of Simon Glass."

I didn't say anything.

"Well, I want to dance with my ear. I guess you'll have to come along." Ronna grabbed my hand and tugged me to the dance floor.

"Not much way I can refuse an invitation like that."

"It wasn't an invitation, it was an order," Ronna said, tucking her head under my chin.

I stroked her soft cheek. "Story of my life."

The dance was over at one. Ronna had to go straight home because she was taking the ACT the next morning. Ronna's house was a Victorian reproduction with a rambling wraparound porch, complete with swing. We sat, snuggled like puppies, swaying gently and whispering.

"I have to go in," Ronna murmured.

"Wrong."

"Young, we both have to get up early."

"You've got an alarm."

"I need a score of at least twenty-six. And I really want a thirty."

"You're too ambitious." I nuzzled her earlobe.

"Stop that." She hunched her shoulder.

"I'm claiming this ear." I nuzzled again. "I think I'll start a collection."

"Only a lunatic would want an ear."

"Then we're a perfect pair," I said.

"Yeah, a perfect pair." She turned her face up to me. "If you don't kiss me, I shall become terribly despondent and fling myself into the nearest body of water."

I pointed to the dog's water dish. "Go for it," I said, then paused. "No, I couldn't live with something like that on my conscience." I put one hand on her smooth cheek and one on the sweetly vulnerable nape of her neck. Her mouth was soft, and I could feel her breath warm on my face. I pulled back and looked at her. Her yellow-brown eyes swam before me. I kissed her. And again.

And fell off the edge of the world.

I picked Coop up at seven-thirty the next morning. We drove to the school and staggered into the library. Coop was strung up tight, his face pale.

"I got to get an eighteen to qualify," he muttered like a mantra. "An eighteen. Just an eighteen. I got to get an eighteen."

"Relax, Coop."

"I can't, Young. If I don't get an eighteen, I don't get a scholarship. I don't get a scholarship, I end up like my dad."

"It won't happen. Besides, even if you don't make it this go-round, you can take the test again."

"Signings are in February. I've got to do it now."

The test monitors checked our cards, peered at our driver's licenses, and ushered us in. Two people were allowed at each table. I noticed Ronna sitting alone, twisting her hair and gnawing a nail as she read the instructions on the front of her packet.

"I'm gonna take one of the carrels. Keep me from getting distracted. Okay, Young?"

"No problem. Good luck, Coop." I edged over to Ronna's table.

"Mind some company?" I asked.

She looked up and smiled. "Company and encouraging words."

"Used all those up on Coop."

Ronna saw Coop squinting at his packet. "Poor guy, he looks like he's going to prison."

"Coop's in prison now; he needs an eighteen to get out."

The test proctor called for quiet, so Ronna shot me a quizzical look before slitting the seal on her test booklet.

The exam questions couldn't drag my attention away from Ronna. When she crossed her long, wraparound legs—well, I reacted appropriately. The proctor's nudge brought me back to reality, and I had to work fast to finish the first section.

The other sections of the test I spent in other fantasies. Mostly about those legs. Yet the contradiction of those gnawed nails got their share of my attention, too. Ronna finished before the bell and swiveled to check Coop. I could see him, hunched over his booklet, his face pained and his hair rumpled into sweaty clumps. When the final bell rang and the papers were shuffled into stacks for the proctor, Coop rested his forehead against the desk surface, his body language whispering defeat.

Finally, he scraped back his chair.

"How goes it, Coop?" I asked as we filed out of the library.

"That was a bitch and a half," Coop muttered. "I thought learning a playbook was hard."

"Let's grab a burger," I offered.

"I'll pass," Coop said. "I want to go home."

Ronna and I traded worried looks. It wasn't like Coop to refuse food.

"Can I get a ride?" Ronna asked. "Dad dropped me off, so I'm bumming."

I'd have carried her on my back over a bed of nails.

"Sure, we'll drop Coop off first, if that's okay."

She nodded as she linked her arm through Coop's. "Come on, big guy. Go with us for a hamburger or a pizza."

Coop slouched into the backseat of the car. "Can't, Ron. Simon canceled our morning run all week. I'm gonna skip lunch and work out. I can't afford to get flabby just because the season is over."

"The season's only been over since last night," I said.

He shrugged and slid lower in the seat. We rode the rest of the way in silence. When I pulled into Coop's driveway, I had to toot the horn to clear my path of the three dogs lazing on the shaded concrete.

"Are all those your dogs?" Ronna asked.

"Yeah, strays seem to know that I'm a pushover. I think about them wandering around all alone and next thing you know, they're sleeping on my bed."

He opened the door and slumped out. "You know, I didn't finish even one of the sections. Not even one."

We watched him trudge into his house.

"Is he going to be all right?" Ronna asked.

"He'll bounce back pretty soon. I'm worried about what happens when the results come in."

"You ought to be worried about your own scores."

"Dad told me I have to take it three times and use the best score. I'll take the SAT, too. I don't need to obsess over every test. Dad does that for me."

"Have it your way. What are you doing the rest of the afternoon?"

"Nothing."

"Wrong." Ronna slid off her shoes and propped her feet on the dashboard. "You're taking me to Houston. To the zoo."

"The zoo?"

"You know, animals—seals, elephants, lions and tigers and bears, oh, my."

15

Ronna told me this was all about fathers. Young's grandfather was a heart surgeon of some renown, but his father was a small town G.P. I think he saw his own shortcomings in Young. Bob's father wanted an athlete, but Bob was the scaredest kid I'd ever seen. I didn't know Rob's dad but, of course, we all heard the story later.

—John Ronald Perry

Sunday I spent the day at Ronna's. We played croquet on the front lawn with her parents and younger brother. The whole Perry clan was as aggressive as they were loud. The crack of the wooden mallets against the brightly colored balls sounded like bones breaking. They aimed at one another and, placing a triumphant foot on their own ball, banged the mallet down and sent their opponents' shooting through the fallen leaves.

When Ronna won the first game, she raised her fist and shouted, "Yea, me!"

"Humility is not your strong suit," I groused, returning from the drainage ditch with my ball.

Ronna's dad came over, swinging his mallet. "Anyone for a rematch?"

"My ego can't take that much abuse, sir."

Mr. Perry's laugh filled the yard. It probably rattled the windows. "I like this one, Ron. Keep him around a while." He tramped away, his stride long and loping.

"You seem a bit overwhelmed," Ronna said, taking my hand.

"They're all so . . . " I trailed off, searching. "Alive."

"Definitely. And boisterous and rowdy."

"You like one another."

"Of course. We're a family. We have to like each other."

"Don't be so sure," I said.

She tugged me behind a huge azalea bush. "Kiss me or I shall become violent," she whispered. She tightened her arms around my neck. I kissed her and felt the tip of her tongue touch my own.

"I'm crazy about you, Ronna."

"Ummm," she murmured, rubbing her cheek against my collar. "You're just crazy."

I kissed her again, soft as a butterfly landing. "That, too."

I free-floated through the next week, quick meetings with Ronna between classes, her joining our crowd at the table and rubbing her toes against my ankle, taking her home and kissing her, overheating my engine on the den couch.

Bobster was still living on the edge, teaching Simon to drive. Coop worked out to the point of sweaty obsession, and Rob twitched our strings by making sure we gave Simon the proper amount of our attention.

"We have to keep up Simon's momentum," Rob said.

Simon kicked into forward motion on Project Lance. The student office workers were kept busy delivering slips summoning Ansley to the attendance office. He lost class time scrambling from one teacher to another, validating his presence in their classes. He groaned about computer glitches and begged his friends for class notes. The teachers were annoyed, and the office suspected foul play.

Lance was just confounded. And it made him mean.

At school a few days later, Rob and Simon had their heads together more than usual. The next day, the bells rang in the middle of first period. Mrs. Parks looked up as if God were responsible. The bells rang in fifteen- or twenty-second intervals, then the lights blinked and strobed.

Deputy Dog came on the intercom, but it squealed and fritzed on and off like the lights. Finally, the Deputy sent runners around to each teacher. After a short conference in the hall, Mrs. Parks came back into the room.

"Something seems to have gone awry with the computer-controlled electrical system. It appears this will not be a 'quick fix' as that semiliterate young man expressed so eloquently. School is dismissed for today."

We cheered.

"For once, I concur."

We scattered into the halls and headed for the parking lot before Deputy Dog could change his mind. Rob surveyed the huge knot of people in the lot and climbed up on the roof of Big Foot, Larry Dawkins's jacked-up, four-wheel-drive pickup truck.

"Ladies and gents, your attention, please. Meet the man responsible for your surprise vacation." He waved down to someone. "Come up here and accept your well-deserved applause—Simon Glass, Mr. Computer Maniac."

Glass was pushed up onto the bed of Big Foot. His skin pinked as he bowed and raised his hands. "I just sort of tinkered with the bells—" he began.

"Ole Tinker belle his ownself," Lance Ansley bellowed.

The crowd was having none of it. First came the silence, then grumbling, then angry faces turned on Lance and people began booing and hissing. While everyone else watched Lance heatedly bulling his way out of the hostile crowd, I watched Rob cross his arms over his chest and smile.

Glass turned back to the crowd and pumped his fist

in the air. "You know, guys, in school, it's us against them, and this time *us* won! Have a goooood day!"

Simon crossed his arms over his chest. I doubt the imitation of Rob was unplanned, but for the first time Simon looked like he was where he wanted to be.

Ronna's mom and dad were at work, and her little brother was at school. We curled into the couch.

"You hate it when Simon takes control, don't you? Especially now that he's smoothing out his rough edges."

"Hush," I said. "No Psychology 101 today."

"Fine by me." She kissed me, long and deep.

"Young?"

"Mmmmmm?"

"Have you. You know, have you ever?"

"Have I what?" I murmured, running my tongue along the hollow of her throat.

"You know what I'm asking."

I hesitated, then the light blinked on. "Oh. That."

"Answer me. Have you?" Ronna nuzzled my neck.

"That depends. Do you want me to lie, or do you want the truth?"

She sighed. "I've always said that a good lie is better than ugly reality, but this time I want the truth."

The image of the camp counselor flitted through my head like a bat. I chased it away. "All right. Yes. I have.

Once. And it was lousy. It was one of those I've-got-to-get-this-done-so-I-can-be-a-real-guy kind of things."

She pulled back and studied my face. "I have, too, almost the same thing. He wanted to, and I wanted to please him. But I decided that the next time it would be different. That I had to want it for me."

"And?" I asked.

"And—I don't think you've ever seen my room."

We climbed the stairs together.

She closed the blinds and stood there. I couldn't decide if she was nervous or waiting for me to make the move. I put one hand on each side of her face and kissed her. She slid her hands under my shirt; her lips moved against my ear. "I want to show you that you're special."

And she did.

16

Doesn't anybody get it? Maybe five years in and out of therapy has given me insight you *normal* people don't have. Those boys looked at Simon Glass and each saw a reflection of what he hated most about himself. That's what happened when Simon saw me. I might be a little crazy, but I'm not dense. But if I'm that smart, why didn't I see through the Lance game? Same reason the others didn't see through Rob. It was something I wanted, so I *chose* not to see.

—Alice Danvers

The next day before class, we stood around the Commons shooting the shit. Lance hung on the fringes, but everyone pretty much ignored him and peppered Glass with questions about the Great Bell Caper. I eyed the crowd, hoping for a distraction. I got one.

Dallas Alice, the school's female outcast, sidled up to Lance like a lanky spider. Then she just—stood. Alice was six feet tall and weighed about twelve pounds. Lance glanced at her, surprised and unsure of what to do.

Alice stood. And batted her eyes and giggled.

Ronna appeared at my side. "Look at that," she whispered. "Dallas Alice is trying to flirt."

It was like watching a giraffe put on a girdle.

Lance got edgy and kind of sidestepped away. Alice slid toward him. And smiled.

This weird mating dance continued until Lance whispered out of the side of his mouth. "What gives, Alice?"

"I just wanted to thank you for the card, Lance."

"What card?" Lance demanded, his voice staying low but urgent.

Something like confusion or even suspicion flashed through Alice's face. She slid away.

Bobster called after her, "Don't waste your time, Alice." He held up the hand sporting his senior ring. "I'll bet Ansley's dick could slide through my ring."

Lance wheeled on Bob, but a voice stopped his fist.

"Lance, is this a new romance?" It was Simon.

Lance turned purple. "Shove it, Glass," he growled. He jabbed his index finger toward Bob. "I'll take care of you later." He stalked off.

After that, it was a barrage of cruelty. "Happy Birthday to Alice from Lance" appeared on the marquee outside the school. A bouquet of balloons arrived in Alice's homeroom soon after. The card was signed, "Yours, Lance."

Lance couldn't appear anywhere without catcalls and crude jokes. Now that a former outcast and a present one had publicly embarrassed him, Lance might as well have been covered in open sores. He stayed in the parking lot until classes started and ate lunch alone. He walked to class, head down, speaking to no one. Alice dogged his every move.

"I don't get her," I said. "Why can't she smell the sewer? She's got to know this is a setup."

Ronna's face saddened. "Why? She's seen Simon go from toad to class hero. She's seen Lance lose his girl and his popularity. And she's got to be losing brain cells along with pounds. She has no clue about how to act. And somebody's convincing her that Lance likes her. Why does she believe it? It's her only chance to be normal."

"Nobody's that dumb," I said.

"Not dumb. Desperate." Ronna took my hand. "Who's doing this to her? And why?"

After lunch Rob and I watched Lance walk past a pickup basketball game.

"I guess Lance knows how Simon felt now. Always on the outside."

Rob smiled. "Nope, Lance has it worse. He knows what it's like to have been on the inside."

I looked at Rob, wondering what he had lost. Besides his last name.

The Saturday after Thanksgiving, Mr. and Mrs. Perry took Ronna's little brother to his soccer game. His team was in the finals, and the game was being played in Houston. He would play two games, one in the morning and one in the late afternoon. They would be gone until late.

We observed the holiday by spending the afternoon under the snowflake-white comforter on Ronna's bed.

"You're smooth everywhere," I mused, stroking her silky back.

"I wish I knew how to purr," Ronna murmured. "It would be so appropriate." She laid her head on my chest. "I can hear your heart beating."

"It does that pretty regular this time of day." Just then my stomach grumbled.

Ronna pulled away, rubbing her ear. "I think there's been an earthquake." She lay back against her pillow. "We did sort of skip lunch."

"You're all the nourishment I need." I said it in a fakey voice, but I meant it.

"Maybe so, but you've never had a thickery."

"A thickery?"

"Yup, a Perry tradition. It is to die for." She slid from the bed, flicked my sweatshirt from the floor, and tugged it over her head. It hung off her hands and hit her mid-thigh. I had never seen anything quite so beautiful.

"I love you, Ron."

She curtseyed. "Thank you, kind sir, but you'll love me more in a few minutes." She crawled onto the bed and kissed me. "Don't go anywhere."

"Can't, you've got my clothes."

"Aren't you lucky? I'm gorgeous and smart." She slipped away.

I tried to grab the edge of the sweatshirt but she was too quick. "And you're so humble," I added.

She crossed her eyes, stuck out her tongue, and sashayed out the door. I crossed my hands behind my head. I was buoyant, and it was more than the high of sex.

A few minutes later, Ronna bounced back into the room. "A thickery. Food of the gods."

She held in each hand two huge chocolate-chip cookies with a center of vanilla ice cream. The whole thing was about three inches thick.

"A thickery," I said, taking one with two hands. Ronna bit into hers, closed her eyes, and hummed in delight. I took a bite. The cookie was crisp and crumbly, the chocolate chips rich and the cold ice cream satiny on my tongue. We took another bite and caught each other's eyes over the cookies. Ronna crunched down, smiling as she swallowed. "You know, Young, this is as good as anything gets. I wonder if this is it? Is this the very best day I'll ever have?"

I traced my finger down her nose. "I hope not, Ron. I want this to go on forever."

But it didn't.

17

How did I know about Bob and the ring? Simon told me. I thought he was just being nice. He said he was telling me so I wouldn't notice it was missing and ask Bob about it. It never crossed my mind to wonder how Simon knew the story. Not then.

—Ginger Donalson

We took Glass to the Department of Motor Vehicles for his written exam. We shoved him in front of us until he reached the counter, where an emaciated man with thick trifocals eyed us with ingrained adult suspicion. As they moved through the layers of his lenses, his eyes wavered as if underwater.

"Who's taking the test?" he growled in a surprisingly deep voice.

We pointed at Simon. "Him."

"Don't tell me. You're his mothers, right?"

"Almost," Bobster said. "We more or less gave birth to the new Simon."

"Did you kill the old one or just trade him in?"

"Seriously, sir. We're kind of a support system. Cheerleaders," Rob turned on his charm, full wattage. It bounced off the clerk without making a dent.

The clerk slapped the test on the counter. "Answer every question, bub. Sit over there; turn it in to me when you're through. Any questions?"

"No, sir, it seems self-explanatory." Simon sat down and hunched over the test. He scanned the test and picked up the pencil. In ten minutes, he looked up, scanned the test again, and brought it to the front counter.

"Whaddaya want?" the skinny man sneered. "If you had questions, you should have asked them before you started."

"No questions, sir. Do you grade it now?"

"You're finished? Turning it in?"

Glass nodded.

"You answered all the questions like I told you?"

"Yes, sir. Do you grade it now?"

"Hold your horses." He snatched the test from Simon's fingers and shuffled to a small desk behind the counter. Scraping a chair back, he sat, his bones making a loose pile in the chair. He pulled an answer key over Simon's paper, adjusted his trifocals, and leaned over the test, his red pen ready for action.

We gathered at the counter and watched. The pen never moved. Finally the geezer grimaced and wrote a score on the paper. One hundred. We hooted and cheered and slapped Glass on the back until he begged for mercy.

"A hundred. A hundred! Geez, that's unbelievable," Coop shouted. "I had to take it three times and use cheat notes to finally get a seventy."

We coughed to cover Coop's words as the desk clerk leaned forward, interested.

"That Coop is such a joker," Bobster said, grabbing Coop by the neck and herding him out of the office.

I knuckled Coop's head. "You big ox! That's a good way to get your license jerked. How can you be so dumb?"

Coop screwed up his face as if his feelings were hurt, thought a minute, and grinned. "Years and years of practice," he said. "C'mon guys, let's go celebrate Simon's victory. Yo!"

"Yo!" we answered.

Simon paused, looking at us, flushed and smiling. He lifted one raised fist into the air. "Yo!" He shouted and turned in a circle, raising both fists and jumping. "Yo!"

Later we sat in the Pizza Palace, staring down at Simon's authentic driver's license.

"That's great, Glass. Now we can put the rest of the plan into action."

"Rest of the plan?" Simon asked the question for all of us.

"What rest?" I asked. "You wanted Simon to be popular and he is."

"Nope," Rob said. "It's guesswork now. Is he or isn't he? We need a way to keep score. A way to prove that Simon is now one of the chosen."

"There's no way to do that," Bob said.

Coop looked up from his plate. "Do you say, 'Hey, guys, vote—is Glass popular or not?'"

Rob stared at Coop like he had grown another head. "Coop, you're a genius."

"Huh?" Coop asked.

"Class Favorite," Rob said.

"Huh?" Glass said.

"What's Class Favorite *mean*?" Rob asked, excitement rising in his tone. "It doesn't say you're ambitious or athletic. It means you're liked." He looked around, his gaze touching each of us, pulling us in. "It's our scorecard. Simon Glass is gonna be the next Class Favorite."

Coop smiled and nodded, Rob's excitement fueling his own. "That's cool. Glass, you've put up with lots of crap, and standing up there with the Faves would be like, I dunno, the turds all apologizing or something." He raised his mug. "All right!"

Bob raised his mug, too. "Hey, as long as I'm voted Most Handsome, I can get with Glass being the Fave."

I met Rob's stare. "You'll be Class Favorite this year. It's a done deal."

It felt like his eyes were boring straight through the back of my head. "I want Glass to win."

I didn't understand. Why was this thing with Simon so damned important? What hole was in Rob that only the triumph of Simon Glass would patch?

"I told you before. Me getting Class Fave is too easy. It will be more fun for Simon to win." Rob raised his mug to Coop's and Bob's. "To fun, to power, to us."

I lifted mine and Simon hoisted his. We clanked them together.

"To Simon Glass, our Class Favorite," Rob said.

We all drank.

Rob returned his mug to the table. "Okay, the man is mobile, now we can set him up for a date to the Favorite's Dance. He has to have the perfect date," Rob drawled as he eyed me. "Right, Young?"

"I have to go meet Ronna," I said. "She wants me to proofread her research paper."

"Sure thing. Have fun." Rob's smile didn't make it to his eyes.

Christmas break approached. Bob's family was skiing in Breckenridge, Coop wrangled a job assisting the weight trainer at a fitness club, Ronna and her family were heading to Illinois to visit her grandmother, and Rob just said that he was leaving town.

The day we got out of school, Simon delivered a kick to Lance's nuts. At lunch the cafeteria was louder than normal with pre-Christmas mania. Bobster and this week's girlfriend, Coop, and Ronna and I headed for the large table that Rob and Glass had staked out.

"Ronna, over here by Simon. I need to confab with Young."

Ronna hesitated, looking at me for some signal, but Rob got up, slick as an eel, and took Ronna's tray.

He placed it next to Simon's and pulled out a chair. "Entertain the Glass man, darlin'."

Rob sat back down and gestured for me to sit beside him. "Coop, do you want my cake?" Rob asked.

"Nope."

The whole group stared. Coop was refusing food again.

"What are you staring at? I'm cutting down is all. I need to stay in shape."

"I'll take it," Simon said.

"Glass man, don't do that," Coop warned. "You stopped running, and now you're off your diet. You're gaining back the little bit of weight you lost."

"It's not a problem, Coop," Simon said, waving his fork. "If people like me now, it's because I'm funny, not for my body."

"You can't change the plan," Rob said.

Simon eyes snapped, and I saw the spark more than flicker, then fan into a distinct flame.

Simon cleared his throat. "Fine, Rob. Whatever you say. I don't want your cake." He got up.

"Where are you going?" Rob's voice was a fist.

"To get a candy bar. Want one?" And Simon smiled wide and sunny as he strolled away.

Rob shrugged. "To each his own."

Ronna, Coop, and Bob started chattering in relief, so I was the only one who saw Rob plant his fork flat on his cake and smash it.

Simon returned, munching a chocolate bar. "Eyes right, everybody. Time for the show."

Our heads turned to the door. Dallas Alice entered, in all her anorectic glory, bearing a pink, three-layered cake. Plump strawberries encircled the top and base. She blushed as she paraded through the tables and set the cake down, with a flourish, in front of Lance Ansley.

You could have heard a mouse fart.

Lance didn't look at Alice. He purpled in combined embarrassment and rage. "What the hell is this?"

It wasn't the reaction Alice expected. Everyone could read in her face that she finally knew she'd been tricked. Her eyes dropped to the floor and she mumbled, "It's for you, Lance."

Lance put two fingers against the plate and pushed the cake across the table. "I don't want your damned cake, Alice." He paused, looking around at the goggle-eyed watchers. "Get lost."

Alice wilted, her mouth drooping into a quivering line. "It's for you, Lance. You said you like surprises. You said you like strawberries!" She plucked at her hair and smoothed her dress. "It was all in the letter you wrote me."

Someone tittered in a falsetto squeak, "In the letter you wrote me."

Another comedian piped up with "Oh, my!"

Lance lost it. He rose slowly, like an engine building steam. His voice was harsh and strangled. "Alice, you dumb twitch. I didn't write you a letter. I didn't send you balloons, or a card, or wish you happy birthday. Somebody is playing a joke, and you're a fool. Nobody would ever send you a letter, Alice. Nobody. You're a dog. An ugly dog."

Alice froze. I think she wanted to disappear.

"You and your crappy cake make me want to puke!"

With that, Lance shoved the cake across the table. It teetered on the edge, then flipped over, splatting in a gooey lump on Alice's shoes. She didn't move. She stood, head up, tears sluicing down her face. Lance stormed across the cafeteria.

"Asshole," someone called out.

Bob stood on his chair and held up his hand. He pulled his ring off his finger, then pushed it back on. He did it again. The crowd cheered.

Glass munched his Snickers as he watched Lance shove out the door. Simon never so much as glanced at Alice.

Ronna scraped back her chair and navigated the path to Alice. She put an arm across the tall girl's back and

whispered to her. Ronna led her away, whispering encouragement as Alice plodded zombielike alongside.

"Why'd you set her up like that?" I asked Simon.

"Nobody set her up. This was all about Lance. I didn't
make him do anything. I just gave him the rope to hang
himself," Glass said.

"Glass, you aren't getting the point," Bob said. "Lance
needs to know it's *you*. You gotta go *mano a mano* with the
guy. Until you use your fists with him, you're still a pussy."

Simon shot Bob a look of hatred as quick as a
snakebite. Then he smiled and got up, crumbling the
candy wrapper in one hand. He tossed it at the garbage
can, where it bounced on the rim, rocked, and dropped to
the floor. "Almost there." Simon stepped out into the hall.

Simon called that night while I was at Ronna's.

She held the phone while she played with my earlobe.
"Sure, we'll be there in a bit."

She plunked down into my lap. "That was Simon. He
has pizza and videos. The rest of your buddies are on their
way."

"I'm past uninterested," I said, nuzzling the back of
her neck.

"But I want to see his house," Ronna said. "And Mr.
Simon Glass is going to get a piece of my mind about Alice."

That was fine by me, so we jumped into the car.

When Ron and I arrived, Glass's parents were walking out the door. I introduced Ronna. Neither Mr. nor Mrs. Glass offered to shake hands.

"We're off to the club for the evening," Mrs. Glass said. "We're awfully glad Simon is making friends these days, but a house full of teenagers . . . " She shrugged her elegant shoulders, and her diamond earrings twinkled in the porch light.

Ronna and I made nice and said goodbye. Mr. Glass escorted his wife to their gray Mercedes.

"Wow, aren't they fun?" Ronna said.

"I met them once before. Trust me, they were bubbly tonight."

"Poor Simon," Ronna said. She looked up at me with an *aha* expression. "That's it. He doesn't know how to be nice to people." She looked back over her shoulder. "He couldn't learn it from those two."

Simon appeared at the door and ushered us in. Rob was with Blair. Coop's and Bob's girlfriends had already left town for the holidays. Simon gave Blair and Ronna a guided tour of the house.

"Hey," Bob said, peering into the refrigerator. "There's no beer."

"Nope. Had to wait until Simon's parents left," Rob said. "He doesn't have a fake ID anyway."

Bob was our designated booze buyer because he had the supposedly lost copy of his brother's ID.

"That's cool, as long as he's paying," Bob said.

"I am." Simon appeared behind me. He handed Bob

some bills. "Can you go soon? The pizza should be here in thirty minutes."

"Done." Bob shoved the money into his pocket. "Back in a few." He headed out.

"What videos did you get, Simon?" Blair asked.

Simon led Blair and the others back to his study. Ronna grabbed my hand and held me back. "Is this the saddest place you've ever seen?"

"Sad?"

She leaned back against the counter and folded her arms across her chest. "A decorator bedroom and study that doubles as an electronics store."

"So?"

"There's nothing personal in the whole house. It's just a big catalog of stuff." She nibbled a fingernail. "I was going to get in his face about Alice, but now . . ."

"Glass was shitty to her, and she didn't deserve it," I said.

"Yeah, I know." She crossed her arms again. "But this place gets to me. I guess it gets to him, too."

I kissed Ronna on the nose. "Go see what Simon rented. It might be a math video or something."

"Aren't you coming?"

"My car is blocking the Brown Dog. I'll take Bob to get the beer."

She went toward the back of the house, and I went to the front. I stepped out onto the porch and saw Bob leaning against his truck.

As I got closer, Bob turned toward me, and the porch light caught his face. He was crying.

"What . . . ?"

"Give me a minute," Bob said.

I waited. Bob wiped his nose and face on his sleeve and tried to get in control. He stuck out his right hand.

His senior ring was gone.

"I don't . . . Who?"

"I, uh, came out here. When I was looking for the right key, somebody grabbed me from behind. He jerked me behind the shrubs."

"What? Who?"

I opened my mouth, but Bob put out a hand, warning me to stop. "Lance. He said he'd ruin my face if I tried to move. He wanted my ring." Bob slumped. "And I gave it to him."

"Okay, let's go."

"Where?" Bob didn't seem interested.

"To the police."

"No."

"No? The guy robbed you. You can get him for assault. You can—"

"No, I can't." He sounded tired rather than mad. "Don't you get it? He wanted that ring to get back at me. If I tell anybody—anybody—the whole school is going to know that I gave it to him without a fight."

I couldn't say anything. This picture Bob had of himself, this brawling, macho guy—we all knew it was shit, but Bob didn't.

"Okay, Bob, nobody hears it from me," I said.

Bob pounded the truck door with both fists. "And I called Glass a pussy for not whipping Ansley's ass. Shit!"

"Come on," I said. "Let's go get the beer."

Bob was quiet the rest of the evening and left early. Nobody noticed the ring.

As I drove Ronna home, she took off her shoes and pressed her feet against the dash. Navy blue socks with little red stars.

"I don't get this Simon thing?"

"What do you mean?"

She had both hands on her knees, scratching her fingertips against the denim of her jeans. "About Rob and Simon and Class Favorite."

I didn't hear that as a question. I waited.

"You said that it will make Rob feel in control?"

"Right, that he can manipulate people to vote for the prize putz," I said.

She sighed, pulled her legs in from the dash, and crossed them yoga fashion. She gazed out the passenger window.

"It makes me wonder." She stopped.

"Wonder what?"

She turned to look at me. "Don't you think that . . . "
She shook her head and stared back out the window. The
tires ticked against the pavement. When she spoke again,
her voice was so soft that I almost didn't catch her words.
"Instead of making Rob more, doesn't it just make all of
us . . . less?"

Christmas Eve afternoon, Coop called.

"Young, Simon wants to go to the Yellow Rose for
burgers. He says he'll pay."

I was going stir-crazy. "Sure, when should I pick you
up?"

"Glass says he'll drive."

"His parents letting him use their car?"

"Guess so. We'll be by in half an hour."

I changed my sweats for jeans and was shrugging into
my jacket when I heard a car horn. I hurried down the
shining oak stairs, over the elegant, but never ostentatious,
Oriental rug, and out the door; I was looking down, trying
to navigate the zipper on my jacket, as I stepped onto the
porch.

"Look at this, Young. It's Glass's Christmas present."

I walked over to see Simon behind the wheel of a
spit-shined, brand-spanking-new Firebird. Burgundy,
leather seats, compact disc, five speed. It was seriously
spectacular.

Glass grinned. "What do you think?"

I thought that Simon Glass in the driver's seat of that car was like seeing a pig on a throne.

"Great car, Glass," I managed, crawling into the back seat. "You must have been a really good boy for Santa to bring you this." I leaned between the seats to see the dash. Cruise control, intermittent wipers, sunroof, and even a radar detector. "Does it wipe your ass for you, too?"

"For all I know, it might. I haven't read the manual yet. There're still some mystery buttons."

I leaned back, wedging my knees between the front and back seat. Coop punched buttons on the dash, changing stations, turning on fog lights, ejecting CDs, and rotating the side mirrors.

Glass downshifted, smooth as a cat's whisker, as he negotiated a quick left turn. It struck me that there wasn't a whisper of the bumbling, afraid-he-wouldn't-be liked Simon in this car. Where had he gone? And when?

18

I hate it when people make me out to be some kind of hero. The others did something wrong. There was a time they could have said no and they didn't. But I did the same thing. I knew when I handed that ID back to Glass that it was wrong, but he gave me something I wanted. Needed. Young handed his life over to Rob the same way. I've learned a lot. Finally gotten smart in my old age or something. Young and I both made Rob into a substitute father. We couldn't deal with the ones we were given. And Rob made us feel like successful sons. Sons a father is proud of. Who wouldn't do most anything for that? Young just did more than I did.

—Jeff Cooper

We arrived at the Yellow Rose, home of the only Texas-sized burger in the state. Three-quarters of a pound of ground beef, chock full of carcinogens and cholesterol. Heaven on a sesame-seed bun. Coop ate one.

"Coop," I said, "this diet of yours is going to put grocery stores, farmers, and ranchers out of business."

"Don't worry, Simon is taking up the slack." He pointed to Glass, who sat with two burgers, fries, onion rings, and a thick strawberry shake.

"It's Christmas. I'll get back on my diet after the holidays."

"We'll have to go shopping again if you don't—or maybe my dad will loan you some of his clothes." Coop wasn't smiling. Shoving his half-eaten burger aside, he wiped his mouth, balled up his napkin, and tossed it at Glass. "Sorry, guys. I'm worried about the ACT scores. My whole future is sort of hanging out in the breeze. You know?"

"I have just the thing to cheer you up." Simon scraped his chair back and hurried out of the restaurant.

"What's he up to?" I asked.

"Who knows," Coop mumbled. "Glass is getting as bad as Rob about keeping secrets." Coop shredded a couple of napkins. "What'll I do if I don't get an eighteen on the ACT, Young?"

Simon bounced in, carrying two wrapped presents.

"Here, guys. Just call me Santa Simon." There was a trace of the old Simon, nervous and bumbling, but as he handed us the presents, he seemed to grow more confident.

Coop's package was square, the size of a box of kitchen matches, and wrapped in shiny foil. He shook it. "Shucks, Glass. I was hoping for a car."

"Open it," Simon encouraged him.

Coop stripped the paper off and looked at the small

box, befuddled. "Terrific, Glass. A Waterford crystal napkin ring. Just what I always wanted."

"That's just a box I used. Open it!"

He lifted the lid and pulled away a square of cotton. His face wrinkled in puzzlement once more as he picked up a laminated card. "Why are you giving me your driver's license?"

"Look at it again, Coop."

Coop looked again. "This is nuts. This is your picture, but it's got my name and my license number. I don't get it."

"On January eighteenth at eight A. M., I will enter the auditorium at Alvin Community College. I'll present this card and this voucher to the proctor and take an ACT test." Simon handed a computer card to Coop.

"This has my name on it."

"Yes, indeed. It do. It do." Glass was practically bouncing in his chair.

Coop shook his head, still confused.

I explained. "If I read this right, Simon has signed up for the ACT in your name, and he has somehow gotten a false ID so he can enter the testing station as Jeff Cooper. He's going to take the test for you."

Coop looked like a stunned carp. "For real? Did you do all this, Glass? For me?"

"Well, I expect tickets to all the home games."

"Jesus, Simon. This is . . . I mean it's just . . . just—"

I took the license from Coop. "Just totally illegal," I said.

Nobody said a word.

"Oh," Coop exhaled. "I didn't think of that."

Simon leaned forward across the table until he was three inches from my face. "Don't do this to him, Young. You weren't concerned with legality when I changed your schedule."

I clenched my back teeth until my temples throbbed. I glanced at Coop, who was the picture of despondency. "Hey, big guy. Don't look like your dog died. I just meant you have to keep this ultraquiet. Nobody else can know."

Coop appeared uncertain. "What if we get caught?"

"No way," Simon said. "The license has my picture. So to the Alvin proctor, I'm Jeff Cooper." Simon leaned back. "Rob said that—"

"Rob?" I asked. "Is this Rob's idea?"

"Sure," Simon said. "He even told me where I could get the fake ID."

"How does Rob know where to get false ID?" I tapped the license and thought that a guy who could change his name might know exactly where to get a fake license. "This looks like the real deal."

"It should. It cost me seventy-five dollars."

"Glass." Coop turned and faced Simon, shutting me out of the loop. "This is a big deal, man. Not just the money. It could get you in lots of trouble. If this wasn't so important, I'd never let you do it, but . . ." He stopped, and his eyes filled with tears. "But it might just be all that's between me and being a gas jockey. So, thanks, Simon. You're a real friend."

Glass pushed a package across the table to me. The paper snagged on the rough boards of the table.

"You shouldn't have, Glass," I said. "I didn't get you anything."

Coop looked mystified. "Open it, Young."

I tugged at the ribbon, and the bow unraveled. I picked at the tape and folded the paper back, revealing a leather-bound book, its pages softly ragged. Classy. I turned the volume over. The right front corner was embossed with the words "Young Steward." The pages were blank. Thick, creamy parchment waiting for words. My words.

"I know all writers keep journals; I thought you might want this. Or even better, use it for your first novel."

Glass had tapped into me. And I didn't like him owning a map of my head.

19

Why did I do what Rob asked me to about Ronna?
That's always the first question. If I had never gone to
that library and learned what I did, then Rob could never
have talked me into it. But once I knew Rob's secret and
I knew, *knew* what it does to a person—then I needed to
patch a hole in him like he'd done for me. And I didn't
think it would be permanent with Ron and me. I thought I
could have it all back.

> —Young Steward, from his psychological
> interview before sentencing

The day after Christmas, I hibernated in my room.
Slouched on my bed, I ran my finger along the cushiony
edges of the leather journal. A matched set of luggage sat
next to my closet door, and a Franklin planner lay atop the
box that held a laptop computer.

The phone jangled. Unconcerned, I let it ring until
the answering machine picked up. Hearing Simon's asth-
matic voice, I hooked the receiver with two fingers and
plopped it onto my shoulder. "Hey, Glass, I'm here."

"Screening your calls?"

"Yeah, I'm tired of talking to people who are offering a one-time-only-chance-of-a-lifetime to put vinyl siding over our brick."

He made a chuffing sound. Simon's variation of a laugh. "Slow around here, too. Everybody gone for Christmas break."

"What's on your mind?" I asked.

"A little detective work."

"What for?"

"Rob."

I twisted the phone cord around my finger. "What about Rob?"

Simon let out a sigh. "Don't do laps with me. Why would Rob change his name? Why'd he say he's from out of state when he's really from Foley? Don't tell me you haven't wondered?"

"Yeah," I said.

I gripped the phone hard. A day with Simon. I'd rather eat a worm. But Rob knew all my secrets. I wanted to know his.

"I'll be there in ten minutes."

"We know that Rob's last address was two-twelve Monroe in Foley. We're going to get a map and find the house."

"Then what?"

"Then we see who lives there."

"How do we do that? The telephone book won't help."

Simon wagged his head in disgust. "No, the telephone book won't help. Don't you watch television? After we buy a pizza, we go to the house pretending to deliver it."

We took the off-ramp that led downtown and cruised until we saw a pizza place that advertised free delivery. We ordered a pizza to go and asked the cashier if he had a map with street names. We studied the map and followed the road to a neighborhood landscaped like a gardener's wet dream. I pointed. "There it is, two-twelve." The house was long, low, and elegant.

"Rob's dad does pretty well," Simon said.

"Yeah, if his dad still lives here."

"He lived here once."

I nodded. "Guess so."

Turning into the wide circular drive, we pulled up to the front of the house. A white BMW was parked at the side entrance. We stepped out of the car and clumped up the pebbled walk. Poinsettias bloomed in ornate cast-iron planters that flanked the double doors. Simon lifted a brass ring that hung from a lion's mouth and knocked it against the sleek, dark wood. We waited and fidgeted.

"Ring the bell. In a house this size nobody could hear a knock."

Glass punched the bell, and the door jerked open before he could pull his finger back.

"Okay, I'm here. I'm here." The speaker was a tall woman in lavender sweats, flushed and breathing hard as she smiled at us. "Sorry, it took me so long. I was on the treadmill."

"Pizza delivery," Simon said.

"I didn't order pizza."

"Um, well . . . " Simon bumbled about. "It says here, 'Pizza, supreme, hold anchovies, Robert Baddeck, two-twelve South Monroe.' " Glass looked up. "Is Mr. Baddeck here? Maybe he ordered and didn't mention it."

The woman's expression slid from friendly to suspicious. "What's going on here?"

We didn't say anything.

"You two are up to no good, but I can't imagine why."

We still didn't say anything.

"Well, whatever it is doesn't concern me." She pushed her hair off her forehead. "We bought the house from *Mrs.* Baddeck. Mr. Baddeck has a new address. He's in prison." She eyed us again. "Go away. This is old news, and it's my house now, not a tourist attraction." She slammed the door.

We trudged back to the car without a word. We got in and clipped the seat belts.

"What in the hell does that mean?"

"I know how to find out," Simon said, with creepy composure.

After getting directions from a service station, we

drove to the local library. I sat back in the soft leather seats, deep in my own thoughts.

After we got to the library, Glass led me to the microfilm viewer.

"What are we doing?" I demanded.

"She referred to old news. There has to be something in the papers. If there is a connection to Rob, my guess is that it happened at about the time he transferred to B'Vale."

"Not bad, Glass."

The librarian interrupted us with a box of rolled film. She briefed us on using microfilm and viewers, and left.

"Here," Simon said. "You take half." He grumbled about this not being in the library's computer system and pushed the rolls at me. "Scan anything that might give us a clue."

I sat down and threaded the first roll of film, clicked the viewer, and squinted at the pages on the screen. I read headlines and skimmed sports pages, court proceedings, lists of marriages and divorces. The lighted screen wearied my eyes, and a headache thumped dismally in my temples.

I was rubbing my forehead when I saw it. I enlarged the frame so I could read the small print. The article was short, no more than three inches, but it answered all my questions. Even the one I hadn't asked. "Glass."

"Yeah, find something?"

I took a deep breath. "Yeah."

I heard Glass's chair scrape back.

Simon flipped the viewer to the articles that followed the first story. The grainy photos, the headlines, the articles that exposed Rob's betrayal and shame.

"I never wanted to know this," Glass said.

"Me, neither." I turned off the viewer. "We're never going to talk about this again, Simon. Never."

20

I went out with Young a few times, you know. He like,
dumped that skinny little virgin queen, Ronna Perry, for
me. But Young's friends all thought they were such hot
stuff. They all acted like Young was slumming with me.
Young did, too. So I decided "screw 'em" and I dumped
him. I'm sure he tells the story different, but that's the
truth. I ditched him.

—Debbie Mahon

Late that night, I sat in my room flipping the channels on
the television, the bright-colored images a kaleidoscope
flickering against my unseeing eyes. I thought about Rob
and understood why he had to control all of us. A central
person in his life had betrayed him. It was the secret we
shared, what must have drawn us together.

I picked up the leather journal, turned to the first
page, reached to my nightstand, and pulled out a pen. I
tapped it against the thick parchment, thinking, stalling.

I clicked the pen and began to write.

"*He looked at the world through wounded eyes. Anything good was distorted, not unlike the image of a pretty girl in a funhouse mirror. And anything bad was made monstrous."*

I wrote all night, the pen flowing against the paper, the pages filling with Rob's sorrow. As I wrote, I began to understand more, pulling off layer upon layer of past hints, clues to the inner Rob that I hadn't seen. I knew that no matter what, I'd never betray him.

Coop had a day off, so we went to the beach to run his dogs. As we jogged, our sneakers slapped against the wet sand. Coop ran, loose and steady, more at ease than I'd seen him in weeks, since he took the ACT. The dogs bounded and splashed, barking at seagulls and running from waves.

"Coop, you know you've got a pass on the ACT, why are you still working out like this?"

"Just because Simon's gonna get me an eighteen on the test, doesn't make me any smarter."

I huffed alongside. "Is there a connection I've missed here?"

"This is great. I'm explaining something to you. Simon takes the test; I get a scholarship. I still gotta go to school, you know. I don't just go play ball."

"I still don't get why we're running."

"Young, I have to be in such great shape and show so much hustle that the coach won't have any reason to dump me. I have to make it worth his trouble to get me tutors and stuff—keep me eligible."

"Makes sense," I said, sounding as wheezy as Simon. "Can we slow down? One of the dogs fainted."

Coop laughed, big and full-chested. Happy. "Sure. I'll run again later. I still need to trim off a couple of pounds." He patted a stomach that looked like granite.

Dropping the gait to a walk, I asked, "Doesn't Simon work out with you anymore?"

Coop stopped and raked his fingers through his hair. The wind pushed it forward over his eyebrows. His wide-open face was flushed and shining with good health. But he caught his bottom lip between his teeth, and his eyes darkened with trouble.

"I don't know what to think about Simon. First, I feel one way, but then something sort of, I don't know, sort of sours around the edges. Like that green junk that grows on cheese."

"Yeah," I agreed. I looked out at the waves hammering into the shore. "I know what you mean. I feel the same way. He's like a big overgrown sheep. He just lets us run his life, change it, change him. I used to kind of like him when he showed any little lick of gumption or fight, but now . . ." I dug in the sand with my shoe. "Now, I hate it when he does. I guess he can't win with me."

"Then he goes and hands me a life," Coop interrupted, so deep in his own thoughts, he hadn't heard mine. "That's exactly what he's doing by taking the ACT for me. I dunno. I see him gaining that weight, and it's like I see Dad in that chair telling me I'll be just like him. I want to punch Simon out for giving up on his body. But then I remember what he's doing for me, you know?"

I knew. Glass was my funhouse mirror.

December twenty-eighth dawned gray and grim. The doorbell pulled me away from a rerun of *Mr. Deeds Goes to Town*. I loved movies where you knew the good guys really were good, and in the end, the bad guys would get it in the gizzard.

I opened the door to see Rob, decked out in a new Polo jacket.

"Didn't think you'd be back this soon. Great jacket. Did you rob a bank?"

"FFO with my grandparents. This was a consolation prize. Can I come in, or do you want to wait until it starts raining?" FFO was short for Forced Family Outing. An entry from *The Book of Bob*.

I shut the door and followed Rob into the den.

"What are you watching?" He nodded toward the TV as he unzipped his jacket and sprawled on the couch.

I punched the remote control. "Old stuff. You'd hate it. Not a high enough body count for you."

"How was your Christmas? Did you make a haul?" he asked.

"Not like you, obviously. Cranky and Crabby gave me the usual savings bond and combination fruitcake/Christmas-tree stand."

"Cranky and Crabby?"

"My grandparents. Paternal. Sire and dam of Daddy Dearest."

"So T. Steward III inherited his pleasant disposition."

"To think I'm the only heir to that fabulous gene pool."

"Forget it. We won't all grow up to be our fathers."

I let the conversation sag. Not trusting myself.

Rob appeared preoccupied and didn't seem to notice my silence. He straightened the coffee table, aligning the magazine edges with mathematical precision.

"When's Ronna coming back?"

"Tomorrow afternoon."

"Do you have a date New Year's Eve?"

"Nothing definite, why?"

"Because you're going out with Debbie Mahon."

I didn't say anything. *Stunned* didn't begin to cover how I felt.

"I'm what?"

Rob had the decency to look uncomfortable. "You heard."

I played dumb. "I don't get it, Rob."

He leaned forward. Discomfort slid into a kind of regret. "You're not going to like this and neither do I. But it's necessary." He paused, obviously searching for words. "Simon has to have a date for the Favorite's Dance. People have to know that he has the date before the voting."

"I see the point in that. But I don't know what it has to do with me."

"Young, if you weren't afflicted with a terminal case of cranial rectitus, you'd see what the rest of B'Vale sees. Glass goes soft-eyed and gooey-voiced every time Ronna's name is mentioned."

He was wrong and right. Right about Simon having a thing for Ronna. Wrong that I didn't see it.

I sat for a minute, staring at my feet, trying to find a way to salvage Ronna and myself without sacrificing Rob. "We can get Glass elected Class Favorite without Ronna." I glanced up at him. "Can't we?"

Rob shook his head. "You said that you saw the point. Simon has to be more than the class clown."

"Set him up with Blair. She'll do it if you ask her."

"Ronna's perfect. Blair is a little out of his league. Glass might date the princess, but he'll never date the queen. Besides, he won't ask anybody but Ronna."

I kept my eyes on my feet. "Rob . . . ," I began.

He leaned forward again, earnest and seeking. "C'mon, Young. Do this for me. You're the first friend I made when I came here. And I've always counted on you. It's not like it's permanent for you and Ronna. Just until the dance. Afterward, Ronna's yours for as long as you like."

"And what about Simon?"

Rob relaxed back into the couch. "Once he's elected Class Favorite, the game's over. I win."

I wanted to say no.

Rob waited until I looked up at him, then he leaned forward again, his elbows on his knees. "You've got to help me here. You're my best friend. I know you don't understand why this is so important to me. Just believe me when I say it's a way for me to put things right. In my head, kind of. You can't let me down."

Trust me and *You can't let me down* were the magic words. I swallowed and cleared my throat. Wanted to evaporate. "Okay," I said. "I'll do it."

He put his hand on my knee and squeezed. "Thanks."

"But why so soon? It's only December."

"End of December. It's only six weeks until the dance. You have to cool it with Ronna to give Simon a clear path. He's not going to ask Ronna to the Favorite's Dance if you're still in the picture. And it's barely enough time for Ronna to get the picture that it's over for you two and she may as well go out with Simon."

"She won't go."

"Yes, she will. She'll be nominated for Junior Class Favorite. She'll have to go. I'll make sure no one else asks her."

I leaned back and rubbed my face as if washing it. "All right, all right. But I'm telling Ronna what's going on. I don't want to . . . " I paused, groping, "hurt her. She'll understand, maybe."

Rob pulled his hands from behind his head and rested them on his knees as he sat forward. "No. You won't,

Young. You won't." His words were measured and mechanical, but his tone almost pitying.

"Why not?"

"Because we can't take the chance. If she gets pissed because you're passing her off to Glass, it's all over. She's got to believe you've dumped her. And we can't risk that she'll tell Simon that it's a setup. Simon has to believe it, too."

What had I agreed to? And why? What made me do what Rob wanted? Deep in my gut, I knew it was wrong. But . . . I didn't have to betray Rob, and I could still get Ronna back. Maybe I could have it all, if I just did what Rob told me to do.

Rob went on. "This is how it's going to work. Debbie Mahon has got a rep for . . . " He chuckled. "Being eager to please. You'll go out with her tonight. Then Ronna will get the news tomorrow."

"How?"

"Blair will call. Leave a message on her machine. She's got one, right?"

I thought of the perky voice. "Hi, this is Ronna. Tell me something I don't know. But, wait for the . . . " And the beep would sound.

"Yeah, she has one."

"Then she'll call you and ask if it's true. You'll give her the impression that Debbie's offering something that Ronna isn't." He leaned back and put his hands behind his head. "She hasn't, has she? I mean, you two haven't done the deed, right?"

I flashed onto a picture of my finger tracing that sleek little back. I wouldn't share this with Rob. I didn't owe him that. "No." I struggled with the word. "No, we haven't."

"Great, no problem. Anyway, she'll think you're a king-sized shit, but Ron's a smart girl. When you come around later, wagging your tail, she'll take you back. With your classy background, she'll know which side her caviar is buttered on."

"Ron's not like that."

"Everybody's like that."

21

Break up? We didn't break up. He gave me away.

—Ronna Perry

I called Debbie Mahon. I took her out for pizza, knowing we'd be seen by plenty of our friends. I planned to go to a movie, but Debbie suggested we rent a video and go to her house. Her parents were out.

We did some heavy breathing on the den couch, and Debbie tendered the offer she was famous for. Making feeble excuses, I turned her down. I could be a shit but not a slut. Besides, I knew that Debbie would tell all her friends that we had made it. Debbie prized prowess over reputation.

I left, depressed and guilt-ridden. Ronna would hear as soon as she stepped through her front door.

Ronna didn't call; she faced me down in person.

"Young, Ronna's here." My mother appeared at my door. She was holding a book, one finger saving her place.

"Okay, Mom. I'll be right down."

"She seems upset, Young. Is something amiss with you two?"

Amiss. My mom actually talks like that.

"Sort of. We need to talk alone."

"The sun is peeking through for the first time in days: why don't you sit in the garden?"

I trudged downstairs, and my heart did a crazy tap dance when I saw her. Ronna stood with one foot planted and the other raised on the toes, pivoting the heel right then left. She looked tense and pale.

She raised her eyes. "I, uh, don't know why I'm, um, here, exactly."

"I do," I said, trying to keep my voice steady. "Let's go out back and talk."

She nodded and stepped past me through the living room and out the French doors. The Victorian knot garden, my mother's obsession, had a small fountain with cherubs spurting water from puckered lips. Ronna assessed the manicured shrubs. "This is beautiful."

I shrugged and avoided her eyes by feigning interest in the surroundings. I nodded at the fountain. "I don't know why anyone thinks fat babies spitting water is considered cool, but my mother says it's enchanting."

Ronna sat down, perched on the edge of a wrought-iron love seat. "I'm sort of out of my element here. Bet you don't play much croquet on this lawn."

I laughed. It sounded hollow. "No, driving wickets in this lawn; getting bare patches would send my mother into cardiac arrest."

Ronna put the tip of her tongue up against her top

lip and lowered her head. She looked up through her lashes at me. "I guess I know how she would feel. To have something . . . " She paused. "Something so lovely, spoiled."

I turned away, feeling like I had eaten rocks.

"So, it's true," Ronna whispered. Inhaling audibly, she spoke again, stronger. "You went out with Debbie Mahon."

I didn't answer.

Squinting in the dappled sunlight, she gazed out, searching the shrubbery for new words. "I hear that the date was quite, um, successful."

Turning to look at her, I tried to assume a cold, disconnected air, but when I caught sight of that innocent, exposed nape, tears started in my eyes and my throat closed. I said, "Well, you never know who to believe, do you?"

"I've always believed you." Not a hint of a whine or a whimper.

"Maybe that was a mistake," I said. Christ, I hated myself.

"I can't figure it, Young. We had that. Sex, I mean, and I thought it was special, just us, you know? Why would you want someone else? And of all the someone elses, why Debbie Mahon? It seems beneath you."

"There's not much that's beneath me, Ronna."

Tears welled up in Ronna's eyes, but she looked through them, straight into my black heart. "There's a missing piece here. What is it, Young?" A tear escaped Ronna's left eye and rolled down her cheek.

I sighed and sat on the bench next to her. "I knew I couldn't do this. And I knew you wouldn't go for the story, but I couldn't tell Rob why you wouldn't believe it. You're right, it was special and it was just us."

"Rob? What's Rob got to do with this?"

Taking Ron's hand, I pressed it against my cheek. "Your hand is so cold." I chaffed her hand between my own, trying to restore the warmth. "You've got to promise you won't tell anyone about this, especially not Rob . . . ." I paused. "Or Simon."

"Simon Glass?"

"Let me explain. You know Rob thinks that for Simon to be elected Favorite that he's got to have the perfect date. Well, Simon has this big crush on you and having a date with a popular girl will clinch it for him. So . . . "

I heard the sharp intake of Ronna's breath. I looked up at her. She looked as if she had been slapped.

"Ron?"

"So, Rob wants you to hand me over to Simon. You won't loan your books, Young."

"No, I mean, it's not like that, Ron."

"What is it, then?" I could hardly hear her.

"It . . . look, Rob needs this. I can't explain why. That's something I can't talk about, but I have to do this for him, Ron. Can't you understand?"

"If . . . ," Ronna said, slow and quiet, "if I asked you to pick between this game you and Rob are playing and . . . ," her voice shook, " . . . and me. Would you do it?"

I hesitated a heartbeat too long.

"You don't have to answer," Ronna said, pulling her icy hand from mine. She stood. "Don't worry, Young. I'll be a good sport. I won't tell anyone. The whole school will just think you're a horny shit, and Simon will have his perfect date. Simon's the one person in school who won't be using me." She turned toward the side gate. "That's kind of comforting."

I reached across her and put my hand over the gate handle. "Ron, don't. Okay. Let's drop the whole thing. I'll tell Rob to forget it. It's not worth it."

"It's not that easy, Young. Some things can't be undone. Whether I go to the dance or not is unimportant now. The fact is that you were willing to hurt me, use me and my feelings to please Rob. You traded my trust for his. You know what, Young, you're not worth it." She sighed. "And you need to ask yourself why Rob wanted me. Why me? I don't think it has much to do with Simon at all."

Our eyes locked in mutual misery, but beneath Ronna's hurt there was something unyielding. And right then I knew something about Ronna that I hadn't managed to see before. When she turned her back on something, it stayed turned. It was over.

When I had agreed to Rob's plan, I'd done it with

only my hurt and Rob's in mind. I hadn't thought about Ronna's at all. I wanted to hit rewind, make this all go away. Backtrack and make myself a better person. The only way to do that now was to let her leave with dignity.

I released the gate handle and stepped aside. "I love you, Ron, but you deserve better than me. I'm sorry."

"I know," she said gently, with a tenderness that ripped me apart. "Me, too." She pulled the gate shut behind her. The latch clicked securely into place.

22

I always hated that whole bunch of boys, the Glass kid included. A batch of spoiled little shits. Like I didn't know the one named Bobster called me the "Goulash Ghoul." If it wouldn't have gotten me fired, he'd have had a laxative chaser in his stew. Every one of them should've had a few ass kickin's when they were little and nothing like this would have happened.

—Martha McDaniel, BrazosVale
cafeteria worker

My New Year's Eve date with Debbie clinched the deal. A bunch of us went to the jetties to shoot fireworks. Simon appeared alone. Coop, Bobster, and assorted others asked about Ronna. I told them we broke up and nothing else. Who knew what Debbie whispered into any ear that got near her mouth? All I could think about was Ron. Where was she? Was she thinking of me?

New Year's Day was long and boring. When I called Coop at about seven that night, I couldn't stand my own company. I had all the personal charm of a pint of snot.

Mr. Cooper answered the phone and told me Coop had left with "some lardass in a hotshot car."

We gathered in the Commons before school the next day, with the usual post-holidays grumping and grousing. The doors to the snack bar were still closed, but about the time I found Rob and the others, the Wicked Witch of the Lunch Line put the keys in the door and pushed them open.

And she was eyeball to eyeball with a cow.

In the cafeteria.

A cow.

A fright-maddened cow.

The cafeteria lady of our nightmares uttered something between a squeak and a squawk. The cow stamped. The woman let loose a full-powered screech. And the cow charged. The cafeteria lady tumbled head over asshole as the cow thundered past. Tables and books flew airborne, then crashed, scattering homework, purses, jackets, and people across the Commons. Those who weren't fleeing from Bossie's path were doubled up in laughter.

Suddenly, Glass grabbed Bobster's jacket and darted to the cow. He flapped the jacket like a roly-poly matador, yelling, "Tostado! Tostado!" He whirled in a clumsy pirouette. The cow, obviously befuddled by this bizarre sight, stopped her crazed rush, then stood, dejected, her nostrils flaring with each labored breath.

Glass shouted to a knot of boys wearing navy blue

corduroy FFA jackets. "One of you goat ropers come over here and show us your stuff. Hog-tie this doggie."

John Allen Dixon loped forward, pulling off his belt. He looped it over the cow's neck, making a halter of sorts, and led the traumatized animal to the door. "What'll I do with her?"

"Grill over mesquite, marinating frequently," Simon ordered.

We laughed until we were breathless and teary-eyed.

Just as Deputy Dog strode in, demanding, "Where did this cow come from?" a message flashed across the electronic marquee that B'Vale has nicknamed Fred. In caps it read, COW? WHAT COW? then, HAPPY MOO YEAR, EVERYONE!

Deputy turned a rich but mottled purple. He stormed from the Commons muttering about cattle rustling and lynchings.

The place went berserk. "Happy Moooooo Year!" was shouted again and again amid the hoots and howls of laughter. Rob wasn't laughing. His face was hard lines and sharp angles as he glared at Simon, who had resumed his matador routine. Glass paused in his twirls and whirls, panting, scanning the crowd, searching. He caught sight of Rob and grinned with a thumbs-up signal.

The veins in Rob's temple throbbed visibly, and he spun on one heel and strode away.

But the fun wasn't over. Six armadillos chased squealing girls from a restroom just before lunch. Deputy Dog, returning from his daily cruise around the parking lot in his single-handed war against parking decal transgressors, was greeted by two dozen hamsters that bolted from his desk drawer. The hamsters, probably scared hollow by the Deputy's croaking cries, left their regards in tiny pellets all over his office.

No one doubted the perpetrator of these animal antics. Glass's back was pounded until he was in a perpetual wheeze. In a few short months, he had been parlayed from hated, to tolerated, to accepted, and now he was practically revered.

Rob sat mute at the lunch table, his expression unreadable as a parade of well-wishers high-fived Glass.

Finally, Rob stood. "Young, Bobster, Coop, meet me in my office after school." He honed in on Simon. "You, too." Then he pushed his tray across the table. "Put that away for me, Glass."

Simon gaped in surprise. But Rob's face must have prevented him from uttering a word of refusal. "Sure, Rob. Why not?"

Rob left, not acknowledging him. We watched in uncomfortable silence.

The equipment room was open when Bobster and I got there. Rob sat on stacked tumbling mats, his fingers gripping the mats at each side of his thighs. Coop sprawled on the floor, a volleyball tucked under his head like a pillow.

"Pull up a mat and sit down." Rob's voice was smooth and controlled.

We did. I sat with my back against a big chalkboard, my arms resting on my raised knees. Bobster stretched out on his side and toyed with a stand of baseball bats. I popped my knuckles.

"Nervous?" Rob asked.

"I feel like I've been called to the principal's office."

"Relax, you did what I asked."

Just then a shadow filled the doorway.

"Close the door behind you, Glass."

Simon reached behind him and drew the door shut without turning around. The lights weren't on in the tiny room, and the only illumination shot through a narrow rectangular window in the closed door, falling in a thin shaft across Rob's face. "Sit down, Simon."

"I'd rather stand if you don't mind."

"But I do mind, Glass. A lot. Sit."

Simon sat.

Above us, Rob sat like some Aztec deity. "I want to get something squared away, here. So we don't have any more 'misunderstandings.'"

Bobster pulled a wooden baseball bat from the stand and thumped it against the padded mat. Thud, thud, *thud*.

"Simon is going to be elected Class Favorite. It was my idea, my game plan. I want it to stay that way."

The muffled thumping of the bat was the only response. Thud, thud, *thud*. The even, unceasing rhythm made me tense and jumpy. "Bob, can you quit that?" My voice jangled, sharp-edged against the smooth shadows.

Bob dropped the bat. It rolled off the mat and clattered on the concrete floor. "Sorry."

Since the night of the ring, Bob had lacked his former bluster. I felt bad for snapping at him.

"But the cow was funny," Coop's voice rolled out, slow and firm. "What's the problem?"

"Timing," Rob answered.

"I don't get it, Rob," Simon wheezed. "You're the one who wanted me to be funny. You said that was my 'in,' like Coop and football and Young—"

Rob cut him off. "You don't see the whole picture."

The shaft of light threw eerie shadows on Rob's face as he surveyed us. He locked on Simon. "In September and October, hell, even up to Christmas, we needed 'funny.' As long as the school was already laughing *at* you, it wasn't such a big leap for them to laugh *with* you."

I stretched my legs and my foot clipped a loose bat. It rolled too far across the concrete. The floor must be uneven, I thought.

"You remember, don't you, Simon? I knew how to make people accept you, didn't I?"

"Sure, Rob."

"Then why the fuck do you think you can branch out on your own?"

No answer. I'm not sure anyone breathed.

Rob hung his head, shook it slightly, and smoothed his voice. "Simon, I don't like to hurt your feelings. But you've lost sight of who you really are and that's lousing things up."

Rob's words wound through the dim room. "Being funny was a first step. It got you noticed, got you accepted. But Class Favorite says you have respect. Nobody laughs at Class Favorite." Rob paused, slid off the mats, and rested his hands on his hips. "We have to move on now. Make you someone more . . . "—he sighed. "Desirable. You've got to come across as somebody who gets the girl at the end of the movie."

"I get it, Rob. I thought the cow thing was . . . well, I mean, I thought you'd like it."

"But you were wrong."

"Yeah, I was wrong."

"Is that clear with the rest of you?"

"Heil Hitler," I whispered.

We waited, the seconds ticking almost audibly. Then Rob chuckled. "Leave it to you, Young, to get me off my high horse. Sorry, guys. I guess I am going a little overboard." He turned up his palms. "It's just that we've got this thing so close to happening. And I don't want to blow it now. So, humor me, and that way I'll only have myself to blame."

He leaned against the stacked mats and crossed his arms loosely over his chest. "Now that we've settled that, let's have a little strategy session. What's our next step?"

Bobster retrieved the bat and resumed thumping.

"No ideas?" Rob asked.

Thud, thud, *thud*.

"Well, if Simon gets the girl at the end of the movie, we gotta find a girl," Bobster offered.

"Good thinking," Rob said. "Any suggestions?"

Thud, thud, *thud*.

"Dallas Alice is out. Her parents put her in one of those loony schools so they can cure her advanced clue-lessness," I said.

Thud, thud, *thud*.

"Get serious. Simon needs a romance with somebody who is well liked. Someone likely to be nominated for Class Favorite herself."

"Blair?" Coop asked.

"I think you'd see the Pope in a thong before Blair Crews would go out with me," Simon said.

"Blair would be good to help promote a romance, but I don't think she's right for Simon." Rob rubbed his chin, musing.

"Ronna?" Simon whispered the name.

Thud, thud, *thud*.

"Yeah, Ron would be perfect," Rob said. "Of course, only if that's okay with you, Young. What's the status on you two?"

"We don't have a status."

"Then, you don't mind if Simon asks her out?"

Not trusting my voice, I simply grunted. It passed for a yes.

Thud, thud, *thud*.

"Good, then. It's settled. Simon, you and I need to find a way to make you Ronna Perry's hero."

Simon rubbed his hands against his thighs. "Young, are you sure you're all right with this?"

"Do you always have to have permission from someone? Does somebody have to tell you what to do?"

My voice was loud and it echoed off the walls, into my own ears.

23

The parole board asked how I felt that Rob's been free all these years I've been in prison. I told them. We're all imprisoned in different ways.

—Young Steward

After checking to see if any coaches were around, we eased out of the equipment room and headed for the parking lot.

Simon took Rob home, and I chauffeured Coop and Bobster. Nobody had a lot to say. I chewed on my own heart, Bobster watched the scenery, and Coop jabbed the radio buttons.

"Rob was really rabid, wasn't he?" I said.

"Um." Coop punched in another station. "I don't know, Rob just thinks it's his party, you know."

"He's really into this thing of telling us what to do. I don't know if I like it," I said.

"Well, that's a switch." Bobster came out of his trance.

"What do you mean?"

"Rob's been telling us what to do since we met him."

"Sort of, but he's never been like this."

"Nobody has ever bucked him before," Coop said. "Except Simon."

"Simon!"

Bob leaned forward from the backseat. "Yeah, Simon. Think about it. Simon does something on his own, and Rob has to reel him back in. Remember when Rob told him not to eat the cake, and Glass got the candy bar? Rob's not used to that kind of shit."

I mulled it over.

"And I don't think it's finished. Simon acts like a whipped Chihuahua to please Rob, but does his own thing anyway," Bob added. "And he'll do it again."

The days crawled by, and if I saw Ronna, I saw Simon. He was outside her classroom door, at her locker, behind her in the lunch line. Occasionally, he drove her home from school. While she didn't look gaga, Ronna often smiled when she was with Simon.

I found myself driving past her house again and again. Sometimes I parked behind the thick azaleas planted alongside the curb and watched her bedroom window.

On Wednesday, the nominations for Favorites were held. In their Government classes, seniors were given a slip of paper with the categories listed. In the blanks next to each division, we were to write the name of a male

and female for Senior Class Favorite, Most Beautiful/
Handsome, Wittiest, Most Athletic, and Most Likely to
Succeed.

Simon was in my Government class. He looked
anxious and tense.

"All right, let's finish filling those out," Mrs. Nixon
said. "Then read chapter twelve in your text while I turn
in the results." She collected the ballots and went to her
computer. "I wish one day I'd have the whole hour to
teach government instead of messing with stuff like this."
She picked up another ballot and typed. "You'll have
results by lunchtime tomorrow."

We did. A sample ballot for the final voting to be
held February eleventh was posted on each teacher's door
Thursday morning. Before we filed in for first period, Rob
and I checked the ballot on Mrs. Parks's door.

"Well, you done good, Papa Bear," I said. "You got
Baby Bear nominated for Class Favorite. However, you
also got your ownself nominated."

"No problem, there." Rob was all smug satisfaction.
"And you, my man, are nominated Most Likely to
Succeed."

I looked at the list again. "Coop is up for Most
Athletic, that's a lock, and Bob got it for Most
Handsome."

"Maybe that will perk him up some. He hasn't been
the old Bob lately. Have you noticed?"

I decided to change the subject quick. "Rob, look at this one. Wittiest—Simon Glass."

Rob looked at the ballot. "Not good. It'll split up the votes."

"So, it wasn't your doing?"

He shook his head. "Nope, looks like he got this one on his own." He turned his back on the ballot.

We drifted into class and I spotted Lance sprawled in his chair, looking like somebody had pissed in his Cheerios. For the first time since sixth grade, Lance Ansley had received not a single nomination. After a fall from the top, the middle spaces are full. The only opening is at the bottom. And Lance had made it impossible for us to remember how, why, or if we'd ever liked him anyway.

Coop and I came to lunch late the day nominations were announced. Ronna sat next to Simon. I tried not to look at her.

"Simon, congrats, ole boy," Coop said.

"Thanks. Where you been, Coop?"

"We were picking up our ACT scores." I had already warned Coop not to admit that he had bombed the test, since Simon would be taking it for him on Saturday.

"How was it, Coop? You look happy, so I guess you got your eighteen," Ronna said.

Coop shrugged, then reached out and rumpled Ronna's hair. "Everything is working out just fine, Ron."

"Do you have any idea who you'll sign with, Coop?"

Ronna's earnest interest in Coop was like a fist on a bruise.

"Yeah, signings are February eighth, and it looks like TCU will make the best offer."

"The Coop will be a Horny Toad!" Bobster shouted.

"I think they call them the Horned Frogs, Bob," Ronna said.

"I don't care what they call me, I'm just glad to be going." Coop slapped palms with Simon. "So, the Glass man gets nominated for Class Fave and Wittiest. Good going, buddy."

Glass flushed. "Yeah, that's something, huh? Wittiest was a surprise. I mean, people just voted for that one on their own."

Rob pointed a finger at Glass. "Forget about Wittiest, Simon. You'll be elected Class Favorite. In fact, I think I'll do a little one-on-one PR now."

Rob got up and began chatting up the girls, bullshitting the guys, and informing them that he would consider it a personal favor if they would vote for Simon Glass as Class Favorite.

"Well, it's boxed and wrapped, Simon. Not many can resist Rob when he wants something," Bobster said.

"Yeah, not many," Ronna said.

"Too bad you and Rob both can't win, Simon," I said. "I have to shove off." Scraping back my chair, I noticed Simon's eyebrows bunched in concentration.

* * *

"Rob, this is your Lit book." I tossed the book onto the top shelf of his locker.

Rob picked up the book and slid it into place next to his Bio test. "You don't just throw something in a locker. It has a certain place."

His books were arranged by size. Largest to smallest. I ambled to my locker with its familiar mess. I was stuffing books into my backpack when Rob slammed his locker door and called out, "Can you swing past my house?"

"Sure, Bobster and Coop will be here in a second."

"I already told Simon to take them today."

We walked to the parking lot in silence and slipped into the bucket seats. Rob waited until I started the motor and pulled out of the lot before he spoke. "I just want you to know that I appreciate your giving Ronna to Simon."

"Dead issue, Rob."

"That was just because of the Debbie thing. She'll come around after the dance. I'll take care of it."

"Whatever."

"You really came through for me."

I didn't say anything. The radio took up the slack. If I had given up so much for Rob, I needed him to give me something back. I wanted him to tell me his secret. "Rob, where's your dad?"

Flicking his eyes to the side, Rob covered his surprise as he sized me up. "What makes you ask that?"

"I'm not sure. We all gripe about our dads on a more or less daily basis. You've never mentioned yours."

"Is it important? Are your parents checking my pedigree?"

"Forget it."

Rob stared out the window while a soft, slow golden oldie oozed out of the speakers. "He died."

His voice startled me. I was lost for a minute, then I honed back in. "Your dad?"

"Yeah, when I was eleven."

I kept my eyes on the road.

"He was the best, absolutely the best. I worshipped him, wanted to be just like him, wanted him to be proud of me. He was smart and fun. He took me camping, taught me to shoot a rifle, played ball with me, the works, you know?

"And when he . . . " Rob seemed to bite back a word, change it to a safer one. "When he died . . . I remember thinking, 'How could he do that to me?'" With obvious effort, he laughed. "Stupid, right?"

I let it go. He wasn't ready.

24

Nobody ever questioned my ACTs. But I took them again. I couldn't right all the wrongs, but I could do that much.

Did you know that Ronna came to the hospital every single day? And she did something great. She convinced me that I was more than muscle and sweat and she taught me how to learn. I didn't graduate with everyone else, but when I finished all my classwork and was walking on my own again, Ronna had a surprise. She got the Deputy to light up the stadium one night. I wore a cap and gown and lots of people came and cheered while the principal gave me my diploma.

—Jeff Cooper

Per Dad's rule, I had to take the ACT again. So I ended up in Simon Glass's Firebird early Saturday morning en route to Alvin Community College. "Glass, you know you have to sign the test, and they have a copy of Coop's first test with his signature."

Tapping his fingers on the steering wheel to an inner

rhythm, Simon nodded. "Got that covered. Coop made a fifteen. If I don't score better than, say a twenty or twenty-one, then the computer won't kick out the score, so the signature won't be compared. But, just in case, I worked on forging Coop's handwriting last night."

When we arrived at the college, we showed our IDs, took our places, and waded into the test. I didn't need a replay of my dad's wrath.

I was tired and grumpy when we finished. Simon wanted to stop for burgers, but I talked him into Mexican food. Chowing down on tacos, quesadillas, enchiladas, rice, and beans was a proven mood elevator.

"Are you still dating Debbie?"

Simon caught me with a mouthful of taco. I chewed. Slow. Giving myself some time, I swallowed and took a slug of iced tea. "Why are you asking?"

Simon rearranged things on his plate. His eyes averted, he said, "Ronna asked me."

Now I poked at my food. "Oh."

"Who are you taking to the Favorite's Dance?" He said it in a rush, exhaling the words almost inaudibly. He was asking my permission to take Ronna to the dance. I didn't know what to do with that. It pissed me off, but the truth popped out before I could stop it. "I don't know. I might not go."

"You have to go!"

"I don't *have* to do anything."

"But you're nominated. You'll win."

There was something about the way he said that, as if it were a forgone conclusion, that set off tiny alarms deep in my head. But the anger at telling me what to do took over. "So what?"

"So . . . ah, . . . well, won't your parents care if you won and weren't there to accept?"

The taco shell snapped in my grasp, and the contents cascaded to the plate. "Cut the crap, Glass. You want to ask Ronna to the dance, and you're afraid I'm an obstacle."

Glass wouldn't look at me; he kept pushing his food around.

I let him squirm. Finally, "Well, rest easy. I'm not going to ask her."

I could feel rather than hear Simon's sigh of relief. "Only because she wouldn't accept," I added.

Simon looked up, bright-eyed as a chipmunk. "Do you think she'd go with me?"

We looked at each other and then away. We nosed down our food, the silence interrupted only by the piped-in mariachi/elevator music version of "Margaritaville."

"Yeah. I think she would," I said.

The ride home was predictably grim, but when Glass dropped me off at my house, I raced inside, got my mother's bird-watching binoculars, hopped into my car, and followed him. I hung back so he couldn't spot me.

He went home. I parked one street over where I could see his driveway from a spot between two houses. He reappeared in about twenty minutes, shined and polished. He had changed his clothes and probably showered because the binoculars revealed damp comb tracks in his hair. I would've bet big money that he reeked of manly cologne.

I let him pull out, travel the street, and turn the corner before I trailed him again. He took the long way to town, around the lake, back to the highway, then the overpass by the mall, and finally hung a right that took him downtown. He turned in at the florist.

I parked next door at the Sonic, ordering a Coke to justify my presence. I was counting out change to the carhop when Glass emerged, carrying a long-stemmed rose. The rose was a delicate shade of pink, like a peach that was blushing. No common red rose for Simon Glass.

I'd never sent Ronna flowers.

Kicking someone else's ass feels so much better than kicking your own, and I wished that I could run over Glass right there in the street. I could imagine how satisfying it would feel when his body thudded against the bumper. I could visualize him broken and bleeding on the pavement, his oh-so-perfect rose smashed and ruined beside him.

As I watched him climb back into his car, safe from my murderous thoughts, I pondered how it must feel to let loose, to allow the darkness trapped inside you out to run rampant. The ice in my Coke was melting, turning the drink watery. I let Simon drive away. I knew where he was going. Tossing the drink out, I cranked the engine and drove to Ronna's. I parked at the end of the street and trained the binoculars on them. They sat in the swing on the big wraparound porch. Ronna held the rose. She was smiling.

25

Coop was a terrific athlete. He had a future, that one. It was like somebody gut-shot me when I saw the damage done to that kid's body. I was there when the doc told Coop he'd have to have an artificial knee. Coop knew that football and college was a thing of his past. I admit I didn't keep up with him much. I knew he went to junior college here. You could have knocked me down with a feather when he came by asking for a reference. His face isn't the same. Even with the plastic surgery, when he smiles, he looks a little lopsided. It makes him look older. But not old. He'd finished school and had an interview coming up. To teach fourth grade.

—Coach Larry Gavin

Friday, February eighth, Coop signed on the dotted line. Coach Gavin had a ceremony in his office. Coop stood between Coach and the TCU rep. Local sports reporters recorded the occasion.

Simon pulled in a twenty-one on the test, the computer hadn't flagged his score, and Coop's future seemed assured. Bobster, Rob, Simon, and I were allowed to witness the signing. We clapped and cheered as Coop shook hands with the rep and grabbed Coach Gavin in a bear hug. He thanked Coach about ten times as he hammered the poor guy on the back.

He bolted over to us, waving the pen. "They let me keep the pen I signed with," he said.

"Coop, it costs about twenty-nine cents," Bobster said.

"Wrong, Bob. This is a magic pen."

"Yeah, Bob, that pen is worth four free years at TCU," Rob said, as he beamed at Coop. "Congrats. You deserve it."

Coop nodded to Simon. "Couldn't have done it without the Glass man."

Simon thrust a stack of papers at Coop. "For you, big guy."

Coop took the papers and read the top sheet. He shook his head. "You're too much, Simon."

"Hand them out to whoever you want. I'll make more if you need them."

"Thanks. Guess I should start right here." He shoved a paper at each of us.

It was a flier with IT'S A PARTY! marching across a banner. Underneath, a cartoon depicted Coop wearing a crown. Next to that was a frog, a crown hanging crookedly from horns sprouting from its head. The caption read: "This time the Prince becomes a Frog!" Below was an invitation to celebrate with Coop at a party Saturday afternoon. It offered burgers and beer from 2:00 P.M. until 2:00 A.M. at the home of Simon Glass.

"Great idea, Glass," Bobster said.

"And it sure doesn't hurt your chances for Class Favorite, does it?" I added.

Rob turned to me. "Actually it was my idea, Young. It will get Simon some votes, sure, but you don't have to ruin it for Coop." He paused. "Or me."

I glanced up and saw Coop posing for the sports photojournalist. Coop was flying high, released from the cage he had been born into.

"You're right, Rob, I'm shutting up."

Coop waved Simon over and showed him the signed agreement, and handed the coach and the rep one of the fliers for his party. Coach read it and laughed. "I'll be glad to be there, Coop, but I'll call first so you can hide the beer."

I dressed carefully for the party, even washing my hair twice, trying to get that casual, tousled look. I got there just after two, and the place was already crowded and cranked up. I saw Coop outside, shoveling a hamburger patty from the grill onto Coach Gavin's plate. No beer was in sight. Simon guided partygoers around a long table piled with burger fixings, beans, chips, and a huge cake decorated in TCU's colors of blue, white, and gray. Blue letters proclaimed: "To make him a Frog, you gotta kiss the Prince."

Sarah Branston and Amy Lawson pointed at the cake, giggled, and rushed to plant wet ones on Coop's cheeks.

Bobster waved me over. "Can you believe this shit? He talked his parents into going out of town for the weekend. And Glass got the housekeeper to come in today and again tomorrow to clean up. Does he have the life *or what?*"

"I've met his parents," I said. " I'll take the *or what.*" Bobster looked perplexed, but his deep thought fled as he caught sight of Ginger Donalson. "See ya, buddy." He dodged through the crowd, shouting, "Back, girls, don't fight, one at a time, one at a time." He was a reasonable facsimile of his old self.

Coach Gavin had finished his burger and was saying goodbye, shaking hands with members of his football team. The kegs were wheeled in as his car pulled out. The party pumped up the volume, and the crowd brought out my post-Ronna fun phobia. I flashed a high sign to Coop, pushed my way into the kitchen, scooted around the corner, and into Simon's study. I stepped in with my back to the interior of the dim, quiet room, pulling the door shut. When I turned, I saw her curled up at one end of the sofa.

"Ronna?" I whispered.

"What's a guy like you doing in a place like this?" I noticed that she didn't say *nice* guy.

"Just lucky, I guess."

She gave a barely perceptible nod.

"Mind if I stay?" I asked.

Looking to her left, she stretched out her hand and twisted a plastic rod. The mini-blinds opened slightly, allowing slats of light to dart across the shadows. "Why not?" she said, almost to herself.

I sat down, uncomfortable and tense. I couldn't find a place for my hands, which had become huge and cumbersome, as if encased in boxing gloves.

I sighed. "I've taken to driving past your house just to watch the light in your window."

"I know."

My tongue turned to sand. "You saw me?"

"No, the neighbors did. They took the number off your license plates and called Dad."

Not only did Ronna know the pathetically desperate lengths to which I'd gone; her parents and neighbors did, too. I knew now how Dallas Alice, Lance, and even Simon felt to be an object of derision.

"There's not much I can say," I finally croaked.

We sat in silence, not looking at each other. I watched the dust motes dancing in the filtered beams.

When she spoke, it startled me. "It doesn't change anything, but I miss you, too." She said it like she was ashamed.

And something inside me broke apart and splintered. "There's no going back, is there, Ron?"

She rubbed her fists at her eyes like a sad child. "I wish I wouldn't cry all the time," she said.

I sat next to her and slid my arm around her shoulders. She leaned against me, snugging her face into my neck. Knowing with a resigned certainty that Ronna was only seeking a temporary safe harbor, I did no more than stroke her cheek with my fingertips.

She sighed and pulled away, rubbing her temples with the heels of her hands. "My head is smart, but my heart is stupid."

Her words drifted in the silence.

"And you'll listen to your head."

"Yeah," she murmured. "I've done a lot of thinking. A lot of talking with Dad. I've even seen a shrink a few times."

I didn't know what to do with this.

"There's just something . . ." she trailed off. " . . . missing in you. And I think it's something that will get more and more important."

"What is it?"

She touched my lips with trembling fingers. "You're everybody's idea of a 'good' guy, but you're not good because of any convictions or moral compass. You're good because you don't say no. You do as you're told and so far, nobody told you to do anything wrong." She pulled her fingers away. "But someday, someone will."

I stood and paced. I needed to pound the pillow in my room. "Ron, grow up. Everybody keeps telling me that I'm a sheep. Look in the mirror. Are you wearing comfort-

able pajamas at this party? No. Why? Because the magazines and other people *tell* you what to wear."

Ronna turned her face to the window.

I paced again. "Bob doesn't buy a pair of sunglasses
unless the hunk of the month is wearing them. Radio talk
shows are a dime a dozen because people call in so somebody else will tell them what to do. Movies tell us how
skinny to be, and the television tells us which toilet paper
to wipe our ass with. And everybody listens. You're even
listening to your shrink instead of your heart." I stopped,
my anger ebbing to a plea. "Why do you have to make me
the sinner because I follow instead of lead?"

I wound down. Flashed and burned, I sank down
next to her, my elbows on my knees, my head in my hands.
I cried. Right in front of her. I cried.

Ronna said nothing and didn't move. When I finished and wiped my eyes with the back of my fists, she
turned toward me. Leaning forward, she kissed me. A kiss
as delicate and fragile as a soap bubble. "I have to leave,"
she said.

"Wait." I placed my hands on each side of her face
and stared into her eyes. Memorizing. Bars of light broke
her face into bands of sun and shadow.

I let her go.

26

The police got no resistance from those kids that night. The arresting officer told me they were all standing like they were in some kind of trance, the violence bled out of them. Young Steward's father got to the station with a sedative and a lawyer, but later the kid pled guilty anyway. The only place we went wrong was letting Rob Haynes or whatever his real name is out on bond. He and his mother both hit the wind. I heard he was in Mexico for a while and now he's in Costa Rica. No extradition there. Bob DeMarco's lawyer got a separate trial and put the whole thing on Rob Haynes and the Steward kid. DeMarco's lawyer cut a deal and he got a suspended sentence with miles of probation. Steward could have gotten the same deal if he'd wanted it. But he wouldn't testify against the others.

—Eric Larsen, Brazos County
District Attorney

The big buzz in the hallways was about Rob's unselfish desire for Simon to have a senior year to remember, by being elected Class Favorite, and about the fact that

Simon would be squiring fair Ronna to the Favorite's Dance.

Monday morning we voted in our Government classes for Favorites. I noticed that Glass seemed confident. But knowing he had Ronna Perry in his corner could do that.

Thursday was Valentine's Day and, while plenty of flowers arrived throughout the day for one girl or another, nothing matched the twenty-four blushing peach roses for Ronna Perry.

The Favorite's Dance was the following Saturday. I was going stag. That night, as I struggled into my suit and knotted my tie, I mulled for the hundredth time that this dance was a mirror image of Homecoming. Rob was taking Blair, Bobster was again with Ginger, but this time Simon was with Ronna and I was alone.

I arrived at the Commons early so no one would notice my entrance. No tacky mirrored ball for this dance. Clouds of wispy material floated overhead and tiny lights twinkled through them like stars. Machines blew white fog along the floor so that feet disappeared up to ankles. The dancing couples appeared to be cavorting in the heavens with clouds above and below. The Commons had disappeared into a haze, and the atmosphere was dreamlike.

Rob and Blair appeared, and their combined physical beauty was almost overpowering. Blair radiant in emerald green, and Rob way cool in charcoal gray.

Bobster and Coop had double-dated. Thankfully for

their dates, Bobster's dad had donated his car for the cause, and the foursome wafted hints of perfume and aftershave instead of the beach at low tide. Ginger and Amy grabbed Blair and set off for the bathrooms the minute they stepped into the swirling clouds, leaving the four of us to fetch punch.

"Why do they have this stuff? It tastes like cough medicine and the girls never drink it," Bobster grumbled.

"Throwback to the Victorians," I said. "Parties and dances were the only time men waited on the women. It's a power thing."

"That's Young for you," Coop chortled. "Always finding something in all those books he reads. I just think the girls are thirsty." He grinned. "By the way, Amy wants you to dance with her at least once."

I smiled at Coop. "Amy, my ass. You want to make sure that I don't just stand around feeling sorry for myself."

"So, sue me."

"Okay, I give up. No wet blanket here. I intend to dance with all of your dates. Charm them out of their silky little panties. Don't blame me when they fall madly in love and beg me to run away with them."

"Now you sound like Bobster."

"Hey, did I hear my name taken in vain?" Bobster said.

"Whoa, turn around, guys. Look who's coming in the door." Rob interrupted us. We turned.

Ronna stepped into the first bank of clouds near the

door. She wore a white dress that hugged her slender torso, then flared into soft folds that whispered around her legs. The dress had tiny sparkles scattered all over it. She looked star-kissed. Her eyes reflected the twinkling lights above her as she smiled at the clouds, then slid one hand through her date's arm and pointed to the glowing crescent moon that hung over the band. Her date patted her fingers and smiled, obviously as enchanted with her as she was with the room.

There must have been magic to spare because Simon Glass had never looked this good. His dark suit was double-breasted and had to have been custom-cut to make him look slimmer. He didn't bumble or stumble or swipe at his nose. When he could drag his gaze from Ronna, he waved at people, chatted, and smiled with a confidence and poise that seemed oddly familiar.

Simon was in control.

"Glass man, over here!" Coop waved a huge paw over his head.

Simon looked up and smiled at Coop. When he caught sight of Rob, he gave a small nod. He looked happy to see me, too, and that singed my feathers. The fact that Simon Glass didn't consider me a threat ran up my spine and burrowed into the base of my skull like a gnawing animal.

"I'm outta here," I grumbled.

Rob hooked my arm and leaned into me, whispering in my ear, "You're not leaving."

"I might be."

"Young—"

I cut him off. "You've got what you wanted, Rob. The voting is done and the results are calculated. I did my part."

"And it wouldn't have happened without you. I know that."

"Then don't put me through this. I can't handle it."

Rob looked around. "We can't talk here. Simon and Ronna are coming over. Let's go to my office."

"There's no point."

"Humor me." Rob pushed on my shoulder, turning me around. I rolled my eyes and shook my head as I slouched along behind him. Following my leader. We threaded our way through the crowds and the clouds, turned into the shadows of the vocational hall, and followed it behind the gyms. Rob slid the key out of his pocket and unlocked the equipment room.

"We need to leave the light off," Rob said, as he ushered me into the dark room. I bumped into the stand of baseball bats, knocking them over and tripping on them as they rattled across the cement floor.

"Shit."

"Be still, numb nuts. Just be still and you'll quit tripping over them." Rob's laughter was infectious.

I listened to reason and stopped moving. Pretty soon

my eyes adjusted to the dim light and even I saw the
humor in the situation and chortled reluctantly.
"Changelings," I said.

Rob looked at me, obviously mystified. "Belly button," he said.

Now I was befuddled. "Belly button? What's that
supposed to mean?"

"Damned if I know. But it makes as much sense as
'changelings.'"

"Didn't anybody read you fairy tales?"

Rob smiled. And I knew I had never seen Rob smile
before. It wasn't his full-kilowatt pulse-stopper, the smile
he hid behind and used to blind people. It was a soft, little
smile. "Yeah," he said. "Changelings. Like the elves came
and switched babies in their cradles, right?"

"You got it. I think Simon and I got switched around
somehow."

"Yeah," he said again. "My dad used to tell me stories
about stuff like that when I was little. He would tell me
that I must be a changeling child. That I was magical and
the elves must have brought me. I'd make him bring a mirror, and we'd look in it. I'd point to his nose, then mine,
and I'd point to my eyes and his and our hair and tell him
that they were all alike. Then he would say in this real
serious voice, 'Then you must be my very own boy after
all.'"

I hurt for Rob, knowing what he had lost and imagin-
ing how empty it had left him. If he needed to fill that

emptiness up by maneuvering the school goat into a social lion, then I hoped it worked.

"I don't know, Rob. You can be kind of magical. Elves might be the reason."

Rob started like I had awakened him from a trance. "Sorry about that, man. I must be getting that Old Timers' disease. Talking about old times."

"It's okay. I might even steal it and write a prize-winning short story."

Rob smiled a real smile again. "Never trust your secrets to a writer. So, the Creative Writing scam is working?"

"So far, so good."

"I'm glad, Young. Dissecting frogs just ain't your thing."

"Don't I know."

"About tonight."

"What about tonight?" I said.

"I know it's hard for you. Ronna here with Glass and everything. I wish we'd done it some other way. I never thought Ronna would react like she did. So, I don't know . . . so *final*."

"Don't worry about it."

"What I want to say is that I know what it feels like to . . . lose somebody that you care about. I'm sorry I was the one that caused it."

"I did it to myself."

"Not without me pushing, you didn't. Anyway, Young,

you can't just run off when you lose something." He
punched my shoulder, then leaned against the stack of
tumbling mats. "Don't leave tonight. Stick out the tough
part and maybe you'll get past it. Besides, I want you here.
I want you to know how we made this happen."

"You made it happen, Rob. Not me."

"C'mon?"

I pointed to my neck. "Okay, I'm already wearing the
tie, so why the hell not."

We kicked the bats aside and cleared a path to the
door.

The band tried valiantly to sound like they were playing music, the lead singer wiping the obligatory sweat and
twisting his face into tortured expressions that were supposed to convince us that his squeaks in the high register
were strangled passion rather than an outburst of
Tourette's. At least most of the music was fast, and I was
spared having to watch Ron and Simon slow-dancing.

"That guy never ceases to amaze me."

I looked over my shoulder to see Bobster standing
behind me. "Which one?"

"Glass, who else?"

I followed his eyes to Simon and Ronna dancing.
Glass was holding his own, surprisingly graceful. "When
did he learn to dance like that?" I asked. "The only dancing I ever saw him do was that jig when he's nervous."

"I taught him before Homecoming, remember? But
then he looked like a buffalo on an ice pond. Now dick-

toes is dancing." It had been some time since I'd had a good entry for *The Book of Bob.*

"Sometimes things change," I said to Bob.

Ginger floated up to us. "Young, I've danced with Most Handsome; I need to dance with Most Likely to Succeed."

I gave her an evil leer. "Careful, my charm is rumored to be lethal."

"Yeah, you look like a killer, all right."

"Hey, just a minute," Bobster said, stepping in front of Ginger. "What is it you're Most Likely to Succeed at?"

"Chew the gopher, Bobster." I grabbed Ginger and whisked her to the dance floor. I called to Bob over my shoulder, "And don't end a sentence with a preposition." I twirled Ginger so that her dress swirled out in a flowing circle.

I got into the swing of things and danced the feet off various borrowed beauties. I table-hopped between dances, staying clear of Simon and Ronna. But my lucky streak ended when Glass buttonholed me in the bathroom.

He appeared behind me as I washed my hands. "Young, I'm glad you made it."

I reached in my pocket for my comb, ran it through the front and sides of my hair, and returned it to my coat. Without turning, I spoke to the mirror as I pushed back the front to get the right look. "Glass, that makes my little heart thump. You know, making you happy."

Simon quirked his mouth in a wry smile. "Young, I

wish we could find a way to be friends. I really look up to you and I can't understand why you've always been so—"

I interrupted. "I can't explain, Glass. I sort of felt sorry for you when Lance ragged on you all the time, but now, I don't know, being around you—Rob wanted me to give you a break. He thought people had to believe all of us liked you, so I was stuck. But, one way or another, tonight it's over." I straightened the knot on my tie.

I watched Glass's face go through a series of subtle changes. First he looked hurt, then thoughtful, then he gave his chin that tiny jut.

"Maybe you didn't want to break ranks, but you let me do things for you. Remember Creative Writing? Maybe, just maybe, you understand, I might get back into the system and cancel the override just like you want to cancel any association with me."

I turned around. "This is the kind of shit I mean. Are you trying to blackmail me into being your friend?"

Glass leaned against the sink, arms crossed over his chest and one foot crossed over the other ankle. While the gesture was supposed to look relaxed, it looked rehearsed. And his foot jigged. It was slight. But there was a hint of the old nervous Simon.

But he controlled it and continued. "Face it, Young. You're not pissed about blackmail at all. You're not even pissed about Ronna. I know what you're so hot about."

"Okay, be the great fucking swami and tell dumb little ole me."

"You're pissed because Simon Glass, the former school joke, has more balls than you. Sometimes when Rob tells me to jump, I do it, but only when I feel like playing frog. You're a frog whether you want to be or not."

I couldn't breathe. I couldn't see. I couldn't think. My heart drummed a war chant in my ears.

Glass went on, impervious, his control real now. "And I'll be able to prove it tonight. Rob wanted me to be Class Favorite because he wanted to shove the geek down the throats of all the socially correct. It's a *game* with him." Glass laughed. "God, you should see your face. Young Steward is in awe, shocked to find out that Simon Glass actually has a clue."

He inspected his nails, his silence raking the room with tension. "Young, the computer is a fantastic tool. It can make or break someone. Tonight you'll find out that Simon Glass is a player."

A disembodied voice came over the P. A. "Can I have your attention, please. We'll be announcing names of school Favorites in about two minutes."

"Sorry, we have to cut this short, Young. Destiny awaits." He pushed the door and strode out without a backward glance.

I stood, my head throbbing in anger and confusion. I rinsed my face with cold water.

With a suddenness that left me breathless, I snapped to what Glass had just said. I hurried out the door, hoping that Glass was just shining me. But my gut knew he wasn't.

27

The worst part? The expression on Young's face when he looked at me. The bat was still in his hand and there was blood on his cheek. And in his eyes was . . . realization. Knowledge of things nobody that age should have.

No, I haven't seen him since. He'll be living with Coop for a while. Until he gets his bearings, Coop says. I talk to Coop often, but I won't go see Young when he gets out. That's over. It was over before.

—Ronna Perry

Everyone sat at the tables, faces turned expectantly toward the stage. I stood in the shadows and wispy clouds at the far side of the Commons, watching from the sidelines.

Deputy Dog stood in front of a small set of bleachers on the stage, the risers covered with glittered cotton batting carrying out the cloud theme. He clutched a fistful of envelopes, each decorated with a bright red wax seal. "We'll start with the freshman class. Freshman Class Favorites are . . . "

He paused for a moment of drama, then slid his

index finger under the flap of the envelope and broke the seal. The drums rolled and crashed, and Deputy announced the names. Spotlights searched the tables to find the winners. I didn't even know the girl; she had long brown hair and covered her face with her hands as she giggled and blushed. When she removed her hands and stood up, I could see the glint of braces; she was lanky and slightly clumsy, like a spring colt. The boy was Lance Ansley's little brother, tall and gangly with a hint of his brother's former swagger. I scanned the room but didn't see Lance.

Sophomores were announced without my awareness. I watched Simon, sitting easy and smiling, leaning over to comment to Rob, as the winners took places on the risers. I looked back to Deputy Dog as he opened the envelope for Junior Class Favorite. I didn't hear the boy's name because my heart pounded in my ears as he called out Ronna's. The spotlight swiveled to her table. She stood, smiled, and waved at the applauding audience as she walked in the pools of light to the stage.

"Now the seniors." Deputy looked down at the top envelope. "Most Athletic," he read, as he broke the seal and pulled out the card.

"Jeff Cooper and Tina Matthews."

The crowd cheered, the spots found Coop. He raised both fists over his head and shouted, "Yo!" He loped to the middle of the floor and waited for Tina to join him, picked her up, set her on his hulking shoulder and carried her to the stage. Everyone whistled and cheered and stomped.

Bobster and Blair Crews got Most Handsome and Most Beautiful. Since they were seated at the same table, Bobster pulled out her chair, offered his arm, and escorted her in a grand manner.

Deputy scratched at the seal for Most Likely to Succeed, opened it, and read out the names. One of them was mine. The spots had trouble finding me, but finally picked me out of the shadows. I made my way through the tables trying to figure this one out. If Simon had hacked into the results, he'd never let me win. Maybe everything would be all right. As luck would have it, I was placed next to Ronna, near the edge of the risers.

"Congratulations," she whispered.

"We'll see about that," I said, watching Simon as he applauded, still relaxed, leaning back in his chair, surveying the faces in the crowd.

"And the winners for Wittiest are . . . " Deputy pulled out the card, as I continued to watch Simon. He looked a bit nervous now, drumming his fingers on the table, scrutinizing the Deputy's face. "Simon Glass and . . . " Who knew what the Deputy said next? Cheers drowned the name of the female winner. Coop put two fingers to his teeth and whistled. It sounded like an air-raid signal.

Glass slumped back against his chair and made a parody of feeling his heart, then jumped up and bowed to the audience. He ran across the floor, snagged Barbara Burns by the hand, and pulled her to the stage. I guess she was the wittiest female. When they got to the bleachers she gave Glass a swift kick in the butt, so she must have deserved the honor.

My attention was on Rob. He clapped a shade out of sync with the rest of the room.

"Now for the big prize, Senior Class Favorite." The Deputy popped the seal, pulled out the card, and grinned. "Well, no surprises here. Blair Crews and . . . "

"Rob Haynes!"

Reality took a loop, and the room seemed to tilt on its axis. I saw hands meet in applause, but the clapping hands opened to faces of bewilderment and surprise.

I felt Ronna's hand on my arm, and I looked down to see her staring at me, her face serious.

"I don't understand," she whispered. "I thought Rob took care of this."

I took a breath, and it felt cold in my lungs. "Yeah," I said. "We all thought that."

28

My son was the only one who took responsibility for what he did. He was the only one punished and he was the only one who never struck a blow. Justice is certainly blind, isn't it?

—Emily Steward

The band struck up and all the Favorites danced together under the spotlights. Since Blair was a double winner, she and Rob and Bobster threw their arms over one another's shoulders and swayed in a small circle. Rob smiled and waved at people over Blair's shoulder, seemingly happy with the situation.

The song concluded. We congratulated one another and started winding our way back to the tables while the next song belted out. Rob caught up with me by the double doors. "Why are you leaving?"

"Party's over."

"Not yet. Meet me in my office. I'll round up the others."

He spun off without waiting for my reply. I hung by

the doors, vacillating. I pushed on the bar opening one door. The cold wind swept past, clean and inviting. I stood half in and half out, wanting to leave, yet rooted to the floor. I took a deep breath, stepped back, and released the bar. The wind snatched the heavy door and slammed it shut with a muffled thump.

This time when I entered the room, it was Simon who leaned against the tumbling mats, in the same arms-crossed-foot-over-ankle stance of satisfaction he had exhibited in the restroom. "Careful," he said. "There're loose baseball bats all over the place."

Bob stood against the wall next to the door. He held out a bat. "I almost broke my leg on this one," he said, and began thumping the bat in an even rhythm against the side of his shoe.

I eased into the room and bent for a couple of errant bats. Rob and Coop blew in. Rob took a long look at Simon leaning against the mats, the light from the hall changing Glass's face into light and shadow. Rob took one of the bats from my hand. "Planning to play a few innings?"

I attempted a laugh but fell short. "Nope, just trying to neaten things up. I'm gonna do the windows next."

Rob turned to Simon. "Congratulations, Simon."

"Thanks, Rob. You, too." His voice was smug.

"How'd you do it?" Rob asked.

"Do what?"

Rob held the bat by the neck and twisted it with the butt end against the concrete. It grated and, combined with Bobster's soft thumping, it made my head pound.

Rob's mouth thinned and straightened. He surveyed every one of us and swiveled his gaze back to Simon. "Don't give me your shit, Glass. Tell me how you did it." Rob was a coiled snake, shaking his rattles. "I know how many people I talked to. You should have won."

"I did. I was elected Wittiest."

Rob flicked the bat out and knocked Simon's foot off his ankle.

"Hey! That hurt!"

Rob held the bat up and pushed the butt end against Glass's shoulder, nudging him against the mats. "I'm not asking again. If you don't want to talk, I'll beat it out of you."

"Rob, cool down. This is getting sort of out of hand," Coop said.

"Shut up, Coop." Rob spun on him. "I'm talking to Glass." He shoved Simon's shoulder again. Harder this time, knocking him off balance. Simon stumbled, then righted himself.

"All right, Rob. Stop this shit. I'll tell you what I did. I built an override into the school's computer, the same way I did to change Young's schedule. Any vote that went to me for Class Favorite was transferred to you."

He thrust his chin out and leaned back against the mats. He drilled Rob with a dark look, lifted his foot, and placed it carefully back over his ankle. "I left the Wittiest category alone. I wanted to know if I could win an election on my own."

"You fat-assed little fuck. How dare you—"

Glass interrupted, his voice heated. "How dare I? How dare *you*? Why do you think you can call every shot? What you wanted wasn't what I wanted."

Rob banged the bat against the concrete. "We had a deal."

Simon gave a hardly perceptible shrug. "Essentially the deal is the same. You were going to make me popular. You did."

Rob banged the bat again. He took an angry stride toward Glass. "You were supposed to be elected Class Favorite. *That* was our deal."

"Stop banging that bat. Do you think you're scaring me? I don't care what our deal was. It was better for *me* this way."

The bat shot out and whacked Simon across the knees. Simon went down in a heap, yelling as he fell. "Damn it, Rob. Stop it. Put that bat down right now, or—"

Rob screamed now. "Or what? What do you think you can do to me?"

Coop stepped forward, his hands out. "Rob, why don't we go outside? The girls are waiting." He edged closer.

Rob lashed out with the bat and smacked Glass's shoulder. It hit solidly, making a thick *whumpf.* "So, what's fat-ass gonna do? Huh, Simon? You want to be the boss? Who's the boss now?"

Simon squealed. "Stop. Are you crazy?"

"Rob, don't." Coop reached to take the bat. Rob stiff-armed him in the face, pulling Coop up short.

"Shit, Rob, get ahold of yourself; you almost broke my nose."

"Keep out of my way, Coop." He spun back to Simon. "C'mon, Glass. Who's the boss now, huh?"

Simon staggered to his feet, rubbing his shoulder. His face was hard, his black eyes snapping. He yelled, "I can hurt you, Rob. I can hurt you plenty. And I don't need a bat."

Bobster still thumped his bat, the thudding faster and louder, like a racing heart. Rob stepped up closer, poking Simon in the gut with the bat. "Sure, you can, Glass. Sure you can."

I didn't know what Glass had in mind until he looked at me. But his look was that of a conspirator, and I snapped to what was going to happen and went numb. "Don't, Simon," I said.

"I don't need a weapon, Rob. All I need to do is say your name. Your real name. Robert Haynes Baddeck, Junior."

Rob stepped back fast. "How did—?"

Simon stepped forward into Rob. He was furious and out of control as he jabbed his finger at Rob. "I know more, Rob. Lots more. Tell us about your *dad*, Rob."

"You—" Rob couldn't finish. He was breathing hard, gasping for air, and swallowing it like it was solid, choking it down.

Glass circled to the other side of Rob, still shouting and gesturing. "Quite a little story, Rob. What I find so curious is why it went on so long."

"Shut up. Shut up, Glass, shut up." Rob's voice was raw and strangled as he spun, following Simon.

Bob's bat still pounded on the floor. *Thudthudthudthud*.

Simon edged closer and pushed his fingers against Rob's chest. Shoving him off balance. "I don't think so." He jabbed Rob again. "It was a big, big story in little ole Foley." Simon circled Rob again and ended with his back against the mats where he'd started. "Man accused by his wife of molesting their son. She discovered it, but it had gone on since the kid was eleven." Simon made that peculiar chuffing sound that he used for laughter. "Mom slaps the old man in jail but, wow, the kid is now sixteen. How come it went on so long, Rob? Did you . . . " Simon paused as if deciding on a word, then, "*like* it?" He took another step forward and kicked the tip of Rob's bat where it rested on the concrete. "Is that why you got riled when Lance called you a faggot?"

Glass looked at me. "That covers all the main points, doesn't it, Young?"

Rob's chest was heaving as he turned to me. "Young? What do you have to do with this?"

I shook my head, denying.

"That's why you asked about my dad. You already knew. You . . . " He gripped the bat with both hands, lifting it.

"Rob, listen to me, I—"

"Don't try to weasel out of it, now, Young," Simon said. "You're knee-deep in shit. By the way, you owe me the election. I changed a few numbers here and there." He turned. "You, too, Bobster. Neither of you guys made it. Coop was the only one I didn't have to help. Is that great or what? The dummy and the dweeb were the only ones elected on our own."

Bob stopped thumping the bat. "I don't get it. What the fuck is going on?"

"You're as blind as Rob," Simon said. "Did you think anybody bought that story about losing your ring? Everybody knows that big, tough-talking Bobster is just that. All talk. Lance told you to hand over your ring and you didn't do jack shit except say please and thank you."

"Shut up, Glass. You're lying." Bobster held the bat across his middle, one hand gripping each end.

"Run outside and ask, Bob-STER." His voice reeked of hate. "Ask what the talk is. And, by the way, how do you think Lance knew where you'd be that night?"

"Shut up! Shut up, Glass!" Bob screamed, his face red, the veins thick and ropelike.

"Christ, what a group we've got here. One is the son of some kind of faggot, another who's so chicken that he ought to be a woman, and you . . ." He jabbed his finger in my direction. "One who's such a pussy that he gives up his girl because somebody told him to. And to think, Young, it was all for nothing. Ronna's gone and Simon Glass has her and all you're left with is shit. Tell us how likely to succeed you are now!"

Simon wasn't done with me. "And haven't you figured it out yet?" He jerked his head toward Rob. "He's not your friend. He's not my friend, either, but I knew that all along. But you! You were so busy trying to keep his approval, you didn't notice that Rob controlled you. He gave you permission to take Ronna, just so he could make you give her up. Rob wants to be the puppet master. He could tell the whole school who to like. And he told you, too."

"Shut up, Glass."

Simon was turned to me. He didn't see Rob behind him, raising his bat high. Simon only caught a glance of the motion as the bat descended. But the bat was too fast, the blow struck with too much passion, too much strength. Simon flung up one hand, and the bat hit it—cracking the bones like Popsicle sticks; then it powered on, smashing into the side of his face, caving in his cheekbone, cratering a bloody dent in his forehead.

As he sank down, Simon screamed, and the world erupted into screams of pain, screams of rage, the thud of bats smashing into a body, the smell of blood and fear. Bob let loose with a waist-level baseball swing. I think it caught Simon's shoulder. I heard a sharp crack.

I backed off into the shadows. I still gripped the bat, but it hung along my side. I was too weak to strike and too filled with hate to stop the blows. I stood and I watched.

Coop screamed and shouted, but the only words I understood were Simon's and Rob's.

Somewhere between the thuds, screams, and silence, Simon screamed, "Why?"

Rob growled, "Satisfaction, Glass, satisfaction."

His bat caught the back of Simon's neck.

Coop, who had been screaming and pulling at Bob and Rob, trying to grab the bats from their blood-slicked fists, shoved into the middle of the melee, his arms raised in a protective curve over Simon's body. I saw Rob's bat swing directly into Coop's knee. I think Bob tried to stop, but his bat had arced up and passed the point of no return and smashed into Coop's tear-streaked face. He dropped like a brick in deep water.

It was as if a current switched off. First Bob, then Rob stepped back. They looked around as if trying to decide where they were. Rob dropped his bat. It clattered to the concrete and rolled. Bob looked at his bat, groaned, and slung it against the wall. Dazed, we stared at one another, at the blood splattered on our faces and clothes, on the walls, and dropped our unwilling gazes to the floor.

We heard the sounds of running, then screams.

We stood silent and unmoving.

HENRY COUNTY LIBRARY SYSTEM
COCHRAN PUBLIC LIBRARY
4602 N. HENRY BLVD.
STOCKBRIDGE. GA 30281